Spence sat up. "But that's why these discussions are a waste of time. We don't know what it's like to die until we die. Maybe the bright light that people who've had near-death experiences see will turn out to be nothing more than the brain's last attempt to stave off the horror of nonexistence." He paused. "It's a pity that the first one of us to go can't come back and tell the others what it's like."

Sandra made a face. "That's an awful thought."

Spence wore a strange expression, as if, even though it was his own idea, it shocked him. "What's awful about it?" he asked. "I think it's the best idea this club has ever had."

Ilonka laughed uneasily. "I don't want any ghosts knocking on my door in the middle of the night."

"But what if it were a ghost you knew?" Spence asked. He addressed the whole group. "I'm serious about this. Why don't we take a vow that the first one of us to die is to make every effort to contact the rest of us? What do you think, Kevin?"

"You are suggesting that the one in question give us a sign?" Kevin asked.

"Yes," Spence said.

Books by Christopher Pike

BURY ME DEEP
CHAIN LETTER 2: THE ANCIENT EVIL
DIE SOFTLY
THE ETERNAL ENEMY
FALL INTO DARKNESS
FINAL FRIENDS #1: THE PARTY
FINAL FRIENDS #2: THE DANCE
FINAL FRIENDS #3: THE GRADUATION
GIMME A KISS
THE IMMORTAL
LAST ACT
MASTER OF MURDER
THE MIDNIGHT CLUB
MONSTER
REMEMBER ME
ROAD TO NOWHERE
SCAVENGER HUNT
SEE YOU LATER
SPELLBOUND
WHISPER OF DEATH
THE WICKED HEART
WITCH

Available from ARCHWAY Paperbacks

Christopher Pike

The Midnight Club

AN ARCHWAY PAPERBACK
Published by POCKET BOOKS
New York London Toronto Sydney Tokyo Singapore

AN ARCHWAY PAPERBACK *Original*

An Archway Paperback published by
POCKET BOOKS, a division of Simon & Schuster Inc.
1230 Avenue of the Americas, New York, NY 10020

Copyright © 1994 by Christopher Pike

ISBN: 0-671-87263-X

First Archway Paperback printing February 1994

10 9 8 7 6 5 4 3 2 1

AN ARCHWAY PAPERBACK and colophon are registered trademarks of Simon & Schuster Inc.

Cover art by Brian Kotzky

Printed in the U.S.A.

IL 14+

For Ilonka

Chapter I

ILONKA PAWLUK CHECKED HERSELF OUT IN THE MIRROR and decided she didn't look like she was going to die. Her face was thin, true, as was the rest of her, but her blue eyes were bright, her long brown hair shiny, and her smile white and fresh. That was the one thing she always did when she looked in the mirror—smiled, no matter how lousy she felt. A smile was easy. Just a reflex really, especially when she was alone and feeling down. But even her feelings could be changed, Ilonka decided, and today she was determined to be happy. The old cliché sprang to her mind—today is the first day of the rest of my life.

Yet there were certain facts she could not wish away.

Her long shiny brown hair was a wig. Months of chemotherapy had killed off the last strands of her own hair. She was still very sick—that was true, and it was possible that *today* might be a *large* portion of the rest of her life. But she wouldn't allow herself to think about that because it didn't help. She had to concentrate only on what did help. That was an axiom she lived by now. She picked up a glass of water and a handful of herbal tablets and tossed all the pills into her mouth. Behind her, Anya Zimmerman, her roommate, and a sick girl if there ever was one, groaned. Anya spoke as Ilonka swallowed the half-dozen capsules.

"I don't know how you can take those all at once," she said. "I'd throw them up in a minute."

Ilonka finished swallowing and burped softly. "They go down a lot easier than a needle in the arm."

"But a needle brings immediate results." Anya liked drugs, hard narcotics. She had the right to them because she was in constant excruciating pain. Anya Zimmerman had bone cancer. Six months earlier her right leg had been chopped off at the knee to stop the spread—all in vain. Ilonka watched in the mirror as Anya shifted in her bed, trying to make herself more comfortable. Anya did that frequently, moving this way and that, but there was no way she could move out of her body, and that was the problem. Ilonka put down her glass and turned around. Already she could feel the herbs burning deep in her throat.

"I think these herbs are working. I feel better today than I've felt in weeks."

Anya sniffed. She had a constant cold. Her immune system was shot—a common side effect of chemotherapy and a frequent problem for "guests" at Rotterham Hospice.

"You look like crap," Anya said.

Ilonka felt stabbed, nothing new, but knew she couldn't take Anya's comment personally. Anya had a coarse personality. Ilonka often wondered if it was her pain that spoke. She would have liked to have known Anya before she became ill.

"Thanks a lot," Ilonka said.

"I mean, compared to Miss Suntan Barbie out in the real world," Anya said hastily. "But next to me, of course, you look great—really." She snorted. "Who am I to talk, huh? Sorry."

Ilonka nodded. "I really do feel better."

Anya shrugged, as if feeling better might not be such a good thing. As if feeling anything but closer to dying might just be postponing the inevitable. But she let it go, opening a drawer in her bedside table and pulling out a book. No, not just a book—a Bible. Big bad Anya was reading the Bible.

Ilonka had asked her the previous day what made her pick it up and Anya had laughed and said she was in need of light reading. Who knew what Anya really thought? The stories she told when they met at midnight were often dark and ghoulish. In fact, they gave Ilonka nightmares, and it was hard to sleep beside the person who had just explained how Suzy Q disemboweled Robbie Right. Anya always used names like that in her stories.

"I feel numb," Anya said. It was an obvious lie because she had to be in pain, ten daily grams of morphine notwithstanding. She opened her Bible at random and began to read. Ilonka stood silently and watched her for a full minute.

"Are you a Christian?" Ilonka finally asked.

"No, I am dying." Anya turned a page. "Dead people have no religion."

"I wish you would talk to me."

"I am talking to you. I can talk and read at the same time." Anya paused and looked up. "What do you want to talk about? Kevin?"

Something caught in Ilonka's throat. "What about Kevin?"

Anya grinned, a sinister affair on her bony face. Anya was pretty: blond hair, blue eyes, a delicate bone structure, but too thin. Actually, except for Ilonka's dark hair—her hair had been dark—they looked somewhat alike. Yet the blue of their eyes shown with opposite lights, or perhaps Anya's shown with none at all. There was a coldness to Anya that went beyond her features. There was her pain, the tiny lines around her eyes, the pinch to her mouth, but there was also something deep, something almost buried, that burned without warmth in her. Still, Ilonka liked Anya, cared about her. She just didn't trust her.

"You're in love with him," Anya said.

"What makes you say something stupid like that?"

"The way you look at him. Like you would pull his pants down and take him to heaven if it wouldn't kill you both."

Ilonka shrugged. "There are worse ways to die."

That was the wrong thing to say to Anya. She returned to her Bible. "Yeah."

Ilonka moved closer to Anya and leaned on her

bed. "I'm not in love with him. I'm in no position to be in love with anyone."

Anya nodded and grunted.

"I don't want you saying things like that. Especially to him."

Anya turned a page. "What do you want me to say to him?"

"Nothing."

"What will you say to him?"

"Nothing."

Anya suddenly closed her book. Her cold eyes blazed at Ilonka. Or maybe, suddenly, they weren't so cold. "You told me you wanted to talk, Ilonka. I assumed you wanted to discuss something more important than needles and herbs. You *live* in denial, which is bad, but it's much worse to die that way. You love Kevin, any fool can see it. The whole group knows. Why don't you tell him?"

Ilonka was stunned, but she tried to act cool. "He's part of the group. He must know."

"He's as stupid as you are. He doesn't know. Tell him."

"Tell him what? He has a girlfriend."

"His girlfriend is an imbecile."

"You say that about a lot of people, Anya."

"It's true about a lot of people." Anya shrugged and turned away. "Whatever you want, I don't care. It's not as if it's going to matter a hundred years from now. Or even in a hundred days."

Ilonka sounded hurt, which she was. "Are my feelings so obvious?"

Anya stared out the window. "No, I take back

what I said. The group doesn't know anything. They're all imbeciles. I'm the only one who knows."

"How did you know?" When Anya didn't answer, Ilonka moved closer still and sat on the bed near Anya's severed leg. The stump was covered with a thick white bandage. Anya never let anyone see what it looked like, and Ilonka understood. Anya was the only patient at the hospice who knew she wore a wig. Or so Ilonka hoped. "Do I talk in my sleep?" she asked.

"No," Anya said, still focusing out the window.

"You're psychic then?"

"No."

"You were in love once?"

Anya trembled but stopped quickly. She turned back to Ilonka. Her eyes were calm again, or maybe just cold. "Who would love me, Ilonka? I'm missing too many body parts." She reached for her Bible and spoke in dismissal, "Better hurry and catch Kevin before Kathy gets here. She's coming today, you know. Visitors' day."

Ilonka stood up, feeling sad, despite her recent vow to be happy. "I know what day it is," she muttered and left the room.

Rotterham Hospice did not look like a hospital or hospice inside or outside. Until ten years before, it had been an oil tycoon's seaside mansion. Located in Washington State near the Canadian border, it overlooked a rough stretch of coastline where the hard blue water was always as cold as

December and crashed as white foam on jagged rocks that waited with stern patience to punish any would-be swimmers. Ilonka could hear the roar of the surf from her bedroom window and often dreamed of it, both pleasant and disturbing dreams. Sometimes the waves would lift her up and carry her out on peaceful waters to fantasy lands where she and Kevin could walk side by side in healthy bodies. Or else the cold foam would grab her and impale her on the rocks, her body split in two and the fish feeding on what remained. Yeah, she blamed Anya for those dreams as well.

Yet, even with the nightmares, she loved being near the ocean. And she much preferred Rotterham Hospice to the state hospital where Dr. White had found her rotting away. It was Dr. White who had started the hospice. A place for teenagers to go, he told her, while they were preparing to make the most important classroom change in their lives. She thought that was a nice way of putting it. But she made him promise to buy her a wig before she would allow herself to be boarded with thirty other kids her age who were dying.

But, of course, she was not dying, not for sure, not since she'd started taking good care of herself.

Ilonka's room was on the second floor—there were three floors. In the long hallway through which she strode after leaving Anya, there was little evidence that the mansion had been transformed into a place for the sick. The oil paintings on the walls, the rich lavender carpet, crystal chandeliers even—she could have been enjoying the hospitality of "Tex" Adams, the man who had left Dr. White his favorite house. *Hospital* and *hospitality,* Ilonka mused—yet the words were practically cousins. The odor of alcohol that touched her nostrils as she reached the stairway, the flash of white below her that signaled the beginning of the nurses' station, and, most important, the *feeling* of sickness in the air told her, or anybody, that this was not a happy home for the rich and healthy. But a sad place for the young and poor. Most of Dr. White's patients came from state hospitals.

Not Kevin, though—his parents had money.

On the way down the stairs she ran into another member of the "Midnight Club," as they had named it. Spencer Haywood, or simply "Spence," as he liked to be called. Spence was the healthiest person in the hospice—next to her, of course— even though he had brain cancer. Most of the guests at Rotterham spent their days in bed, or at least in their rooms, but Spence was always up and wandering about. He was on the thin side—actually, *everyone* at the hospice was on the thin side, or just plain emaciated—with wavy brown hair and one of those half smiles that was suspiciously close to a smirk forever etched on his face. He was the joker in the group—every group needed one—and his energy was contagious, even for teens who had painkillers trickling through their bloodstreams. His face was as wild as his stories. It was a rare night when a dozen people didn't get blown away in a Spencer Haywood tale. Ilonka loved being with him because he never talked as if he was going to die.

"My favorite Polish girl," he said as they stopped together on the stairway above the nurses' station. He had an open envelope in his right hand, a sheet covered with minute handwriting in the other. "I was looking for you," he said.

"You have a friend who wants to sell me life insurance," she said.

He laughed. "Life and medical. He's a moron. Hey, how are you doing today? Want to go to Hawaii?"

"My bags are packed. Let's go. How are you doing?"

"Schratter just gave me a couple grams twenty minutes ago so I'm not even sure if I still have a head on my shoulders, which is a great way to feel."

"A couple grams" was two grams of morphine, a strong dose. Spence may have been able to walk about, but without heavy drugs he got horrible headaches. Schratter was head nurse of the day shift. She had a backside as broad as the moon, and hands that shook like the California coast on a bad day. When Schratter gave you a shot, you usually needed stitches afterward. Ilonka nodded toward his letter.

"Is it from Caroline?" she asked. Caroline was his devoted girlfriend—she wrote practically every day. Spence often read her letters in the group and it was their opinion that Caroline had to be the horniest chick alive. Spence nodded with excitement.

"There's a possibility she might visit next month. She lives in California, you know. She can't afford to fly but she thinks she can take the train up."

A month was a long time at Rotterham Hospice. Most of the patients were there less than a month before they died. But Ilonka thought it would be in bad taste to suggest the girl come earlier.

"From what you've told us about her," Ilonka said, "you'll need transfusions of all your vital fluids after her visit."

Spence grinned at the prospect. "Some fluids it's a joy to have to replenish. Hey, I've got to tell you why I wanted you. Kevin is looking for you."

Her heart skipped—so high it almost crashlanded. "Really?" she asked casually. "What for?"

"I don't know. He told me if I saw you to give you the message."

"He knows my room number. He could have come to get me."

"I don't think he's feeling very good today," Spence said.

"Oh." Kevin had not looked well the previous night. He had leukemia and had fallen out of remission three times, which was all the doctors said was allowed. Three strikes and you were out. Yet, like herself, she couldn't imagine Kevin dying. Not her Kevin. "I'll stop at his room and see what he wants," she said.

"You might want to wait till later," Spence said. "I think his girlfriend is there now. You know Kathy?"

Now her heart did crash-land. "I know Kathy," she muttered.

Spence noted her change of tone. Anya was wrong: no one in the Midnight Club was an idiot, especially not Spence. "She's an airhead, don't you think?" he asked. "She's a cheerleader."

"I don't think the two are always synonymous." Ilonka shrugged. "She's pretty."

"Not as pretty as you."

"That goes without saying." She paused. "Will you be there tonight?"

"Like I have a dozen other pressing engagements. Yeah, I have a killer story ready for our meeting. You'll love it, it's completely disgusting. How about you?"

Ilonka continued to think of Kevin, of Kathy, and of herself. "I have a story to tell," she said softly.

They bid each other farewell and Ilonka continued on her way. But when she reached the bottom of the stairs she turned away from the nurses' station because Schratter would get on her case about taking something stronger. All Ilonka used to control her pain was Tylenol 3—a combination of Tylenol and codeine, lightweight stuff compared to what the others were swallowing. Ilonka did have pain, almost continuously, a burning in her lower abdomen, a cramping. She felt a cramp forming as she strode toward Kevin's bedroom, thinking what it would be like to see him with *her*.

But Kevin wasn't in the room he shared with

Spence. There was nothing of him in there except six of his paintings, science-fiction scenes of star systems in collapse and ringed planets spinning through jeweled nebula. Kevin's work was good enough to be on the covers of the best science-fiction novels—easy. Ilonka didn't know if he painted anything since he had come to Rotterham. She didn't know if he had brought his paints, or even a sketchpad. Kevin didn't talk much about his art, although all the others agreed he was a genius.

There was one painting of his—a blue star, set in a misty star field—that caught her attention. It had done so in the past as well, the few times she had come to his room, and it was odd because it was the simplest of his works, and yet it filled her with—what? She wasn't even sure what the emotion was—hope, maybe. The star shone so enchantingly blue, as if he had painted it not with oil but with light itself.

Ilonka left Kevin's and headed for the waiting room located near the entrance of Rotterham, knowing she was making a mistake but unable to stop herself. She didn't want to see Kathy—the very thought of the meeting made her ill—and yet she felt compelled to face the girl again. As if to see why Kevin preferred the cheerleader to her. Of course, the comparison was ridiculous, apples to oranges. Kathy was healthy and beautiful. Ilonka was sick and—well, beautiful, too. Really, Ilonka thought, Kevin was a fool. She didn't know why she loved him so.

Yet she did know why.

She thought she did.

It had to do with the past. The ancient past.

Ilonka found Kathy sitting alone in the waiting room. The girl could have been cut out from the summer casual-wear section of the paper, even dressed in warm clothes. Her long hair was so blond her ancestors must have migrated from the beaches of California. She probably wore suntan lotion to bed. Yeah, she looked healthy, so fresh she could have just been picked from a tree in Orange County. And worst of all she was reading a copy of *People* magazine, a weekly issue Ilonka equated with the Satanic Bible for its depth of insight. Kathy looked up and smiled at her with teeth that had probably never bitten into anything unnatural.

"Hi, I'm Kathy Anderson," Kathy said. "Didn't I meet you here last time?"

"Yes. My name is Ilonka Pawluk."

Kathy set aside her magazine and folded her legs, covered in gray slacks that had never been on sale. Kathy's parents had money, too, Ilonka knew. Her sweater was green, thick over her large breasts.

"That's an interesting name," she said. "What is it?"

"'Ilonka' is Hungarian, but my mother and father were Polish."

"Were you born in Poland?"

"Yes."

Kathy nodded. "I thought you had an accent."

"I left Poland when I was eight months old."

Her comment was designed to make Kathy feel stupid, but the girl was so unaware she didn't notice. Also, Ilonka had been told by others that she *did* have an accent—understandable since her mother had mainly spoken Polish at home before she had died. Ilonka had never known her father. He had disappeared before she'd left Poland.

"Where did you grow up?" Kathy asked.

"Seattle. You're from Portland?"

"Yes. I go to the same high school as Kevin." Kathy glanced about. "Does he know I'm here?"

"I think so. I can check if you'd like."

"Would you please?" Kathy shivered and lost her happy face. "I have to admit this isn't my favorite place to be. I'll be glad when Kevin's better and able to come home."

Ilonka almost laughed, and she would have if she hadn't been so close to crying. She wanted to shout at the girl. He isn't coming home. He's not your boyfriend. He belongs to us now. We're the only friends he really has, the only ones who understand what he is going through.

He belongs to me.

But she didn't say anything because Kevin would be upset.

"I hope it's soon," she said, turning to leave.

It was at that moment that Kevin came through the door.

Seeing Kevin, even seeing him every day, it was always his eyes that drew her attention. They were brown, large and round, powerful without being intimidating. They sparkled with humor as well as intelligence. The rest of him wasn't too bad, either, even though he looked terribly ill. His hair was

14

brown and curly, soft as an infant's, despite the hint of gray that had crept into it in the last two weeks. She didn't know how it had survived the rigors of chemo, which she knew he'd been through, but perhaps he had lost the hair and it had grown back. She'd never had the nerve to ask, thinking it would draw attention to her wig.

Kevin had been a track star only six months earlier, the past spring, and he had the build for it, broad shoulders, long firm legs. She heard he'd come in third in the mile in the state championships, and occasionally he talked about the Olympics and great runners he admired. He also talked about painters he admired—Da Vinci and Raphael and van Gogh. That he was both an artist and an athlete intrigued her.

Yet neither of these was the reason she loved him. It had to do with something that couldn't be seen, something that couldn't even be talked about. Yet, perhaps, it could be remembered. She did indeed have an interesting story ready for that night's meeting of the Midnight Club.

She remembered her first meeting with Kevin. She had been at the hospice two days before he arrived. She had found him sitting in the study by a roaring fire, wrapped in a red flannel robe and curled up in a chair with a book on his lap. She hadn't known at the time but, with his condition, he was sensitive to the cold. Spence, who shared a room with him, often joked that Kevin must be preparing them both for the fires of hell with the temperature he kept in their room.

Anyway, he looked over as she had entered the room, and she never forgot how his eyes just stuck to her face, and how hers had done the same. They must have stared at each other for a good minute before either spoke. In that minute Ilonka both found and lost something precious, a friend more dear than all the gems in all the wide world. "Found" because she had loved him at first sight, and "lost" because he was obviously a patient and was presumably going to die. He had said the first words.

"Do I know you?"

She had smiled. "Yes."

She smiled as he entered the waiting room now. He had on the same red flannel robe—his favorite —under a dark blue down coat. He had on black boots as well, and she worried that he planned to go outside. His face was gaunt, his color poor. He looked sicker than he had the previous night, and even then she was anxious when she said good night that she might not see him again. He didn't smile as he usually did when he saw her but coughed instead. Behind her she could hear Kathy getting up.

"Ilonka," he said. "What are you doing here? Hi, Kathy."

"Kevin," Kathy said, her voice strained. It was obvious the sight of him shocked her.

"I heard you were looking for me," Ilonka said. "I came looking for you."

He moved farther into the room, his walk unsteady. She wanted to reach out a helping hand but

16

didn't know how he would react, especially with Kathy so close. Kevin was for the most part easygoing, but she had noted on a couple of occasions that he was sensitive to embarrassment.

"I wanted to talk to you about a couple of things," he said. "But we can talk later." He stepped past her and turned his attention to Kathy, and the simple act was like a sword in Ilonka's side. "How was the drive up?" he asked his girlfriend.

Kathy forced a grin, failing to erase the fear in her eyes. She was not a complete fool. She could see how sick he was. Ilonka stood there for a moment feeling completely unwanted. She watched as they hugged, as they kissed. Kathy took his hand and led him toward the front door. It was then that Ilonka wanted to run after him and zip his coat up all the way, and fix his scarf, and tell him how much she loved him, and ask why he didn't love her and what was he doing with this girl who didn't love him. But instead she fled from the waiting room.

A few minutes later she was at the opposite end of the hospice in an empty room that was small and could have been a nursery before the mansion was converted. Here the windows looked directly out over the wide grassy lawn that led to the ocean cliff. The waves were a fury today, the foam splashing thirty feet in the air each time a swell pounded the rocks. Hand in hand, Kathy and Kevin walked toward the cliff, their hair tossing in the cold wind. Kevin looked so thin that Ilonka thought he might blow away.

"If you let him get wet he'll get pneumonia," she

muttered. "Then he'll die and it will be your fault."
She added, "Bitch."

"Ilonka," a voice spoke at her back.

Ilonka whirled. It was Dr. White, her benefactor
and the head boss. Dr. White had the perfect name
because his neat mustache and beard were as white
as first snow and his round pink features made him
look like a good old country doctor, if not Santa
Claus himself. He never wore white, as most doctors did, but dark wool suits, gray and blue, and
tweed hats outside that complemented the sturdy
wooden cane he was never without. He limped into
the room now, hatless, cane in hand, and sat on an
easy chair that had been set near the foot of the bed
that took up a good part of the room, sighing with
relief as he did so. His right leg was badly arthritic.
He had broken it as a young man, he told her, while
running from the bulls in Pamplona. He removed
his gold-rimmed glasses and gestured for her to
have a seat on the bed. His arrival had startled her
and she wondered if he had caught her swearing at
Kathy. She sat down.

"How are you, Ilonka?" he asked. He was always
kind to her, going out of his way to get her anything
she needed. With so many patients under his care,
she didn't know why she deserved his special
attention, and yet she was grateful for it. Only the
day before Dr. White had brought her a bag of
books from a used-book store in Seattle. He knew
how much she loved to read.

"I'm feeling great," she said, though she had to
fight to keep her voice steady. Her grief over seeing

18

Kevin with Kathy continued to burn inside her, like a second cancer. "How are you, Dr. White?"

He set his cane aside. "I'm the same as I always am: happy I can help you young people, and frustrated I cannot help more." He sighed once more. "I was just at State in Seattle and I met a girl about your age who could have benefited from being here. But I had to turn her down because we have no more room."

"What about this room?" Ilonka asked.

"There will be two extra beds in here by tomorrow morning, and then three new patients I already promised places." He shrugged. "But it is an ongoing problem. I don't want to trouble you with it." He paused and cleared his throat. "I came here to talk to you about the test you wanted me to schedule for you tomorrow."

"Yes. Have you scheduled it?"

"Yes, I have. But I was wondering if you want to put yourself through it. You know these magnetic resonance scans take forever and you have to stay cooped up in that narrow box."

Ilonka felt a lump in her throat to go with the hole in her heart. It was not turning out to be a good day. "Are you suggesting that the test might be a waste of time? I really am feeling better. I think my tumors are definitely decreasing in size. I've been taking all the herbs I asked you to get for me: Chaparral, Red Clove, Pardo Arco. I've read all the literature on them. They do work in a lot of cases, especially with cancers like mine."

Dr. White hesitated before speaking, yet his eyes

didn't leave her face. He was used to dealing with difficult cases and didn't flinch about confronting them directly. Really, she was breaking the fundamental agreement of a hospice by requesting additional tests. A hospice was a place to go to die with as much comfort and dignity as possible. It was not a hospital where you went expecting to get well. He had told her as much when he had brought her to Rotterham.

"But, Ilonka," he said gently, "your cancer had already spread through much of your abdomen before you started on the herbs. Now, I am not knocking natural treatments—in many cases they have produced excellent results. But in those cases it has almost always been when the disease is in its early stages."

"*Almost* always," she countered. "Not always."

"The human body is the most complex organism in all creation. It doesn't always behave as we expect. Yet I feel tomorrow's test will be an unnecessary hardship for you."

"Is the test expensive? Will you have to pay for it personally?"

Dr. White waved his hand. "I am happy to pay for anything that will make you feel better. Money is not the issue here. Your well-being is."

"But how do you know that I'm not better? Only I know how I feel, and I tell you the tumors have shrunk."

Dr. White nodded. "Very well, let me examine you."

"Now? Here?"

"The door is closed. We are alone. I want to do a gross examination of the abdominal area. Before you came here I could feel the tumors with my fingers. I want to see if I can feel them still." Dr. White moved to his feet. "Please pull up your shirt and unbutton your pants. You can lie back on the bed as I examine you."

Ilonka reluctantly reached for her pants button. "But this will be a superficial examination. We have to see inside me to know what's really going on."

"True. But at least it will give us an idea. Come, Ilonka, I'm not going to hurt you. Lie down and let's see what we have."

Ilonka undid her pants and pulled up her shirt. She carefully eased herself back onto the bed. The strength had gone out of her stomach muscles; it hurt to flop back. Dr. White sat beside her on the bed and touched her near her belly button, his fingers spreading out, probing. His hands were warm—as always, he had the healing touch—yet the contact made her stiffen.

"Not so hard," she whispered.

"I scarcely touched you," he said.

She drew in a sharp breath. "You're right, it's fine. It doesn't hurt that much. Not really at all."

"But the area is very sensitive." His fingers probed lower, over her scars. She had been operated on three times, and the last incision had yet to heal. His fingers could have been scraping raw nerve.

"I pulled a muscle there the other day, I think."

"I want to press down here a little." His hands

were midway between her belly button and her genitals, just below her last scar.

She was sweating. "Do you have to?"

"Breathe slowly and deeply."

"Ouch!"

"Sorry. Did I hurt you?"

"No. I'm fine. How does it feel?"

"Very lumpy. Very stiff."

She forced a laugh as a drop of perspiration fell into her eye. "You wouldn't be any better off if they had cut into you as many times as they cut into me."

Dr. White got up. "You can pull up your pants." He turned his back to her and returned to his chair. But he did not sit down. He picked up his cane instead and leaned on it. He waited while she put her clothes back together. Finally he repeated, "The area is very sensitive."

"But the muscle tissue has been cut and sewn together many times. Naturally it is sensitive. Can you really tell the difference between a lumpy muscle and a tumor?"

"Yes. The tumors are still there, Ilonka."

That took her back a step, about a hundred of them. She nodded weakly. "I know that. I didn't say they weren't. I'm just saying that they're smaller, and I believe a scan of the area will bear that out."

"If you honestly feel you need the test I will take you to the hospital tomorrow."

She held his eye. "You feel it will be a waste of time?"

"I feel it will be an unnecessary hardship for you."

"I want the test." She stared out the window.

Dr. White did not respond immediately. He glanced out the window, too, in the direction Kathy and Kevin had walked. The two young lovebirds were not visible at the moment, and for that Ilonka was grateful. She glanced at the doctor. There was a faraway look in his eyes.

"Did I ever tell you you remind me of my daughter?" he said.

"No. I didn't know you had a daughter. What's her name?"

"Jessica. Jessie." He tapped his cane against his right foot, as if forcing himself to return to the present. "I'll come for you at ten o'clock. Maybe we can go to McDonald's afterward."

She didn't want to tell him that she was avoiding junk food. "Thank you, that would be wonderful."

He turned. "Goodbye, Ilonka."

"You take care of yourself, Dr. White."

When he was gone Ilonka went once more to the window to search for Kathy and Kevin. It was as if they had wandered too close to the edge of the cliff and fallen and been swept out to sea. She couldn't find a trace of them anywhere. Yet she wasn't really worried for their safety. Kathy was young, pretty, and rich. She had much to live for and wouldn't take unnecessary chances.

Ilonka headed back to her room. Along the way she stopped at the nurses' station and asked Schratter for Tylenol 3. Her abdomen hurt where

Dr. White had touched it. Everything hurt, especially her soul. Schratter gave her a half-dozen pills and asked if she wanted anything stronger. But Ilonka shook her head because she wasn't like the others—she didn't need hard narcotics. Yet when she was in her room, lying on her bed not far from the dozing Anya, she tossed all six of the pills in her mouth and chased them down with a glass of water. She usually took only two at a time. The pills took anywhere from twenty to thirty minutes to take effect. She lay back and closed her eyes. It was four in the afternoon. She would sleep for a few hours and then wake up, fresh for another meeting of the Midnight Club. It was all she had to look forward to.

Before she passed out she prayed she would dream of the Master.

And he did come to her, later, and told her many things.

But it was only a dream. Maybe.

CHAPTER II

IT WAS SANDRA CROSS WHO AWAKENED ILONKA
Pawluk, and not Anya Zimmerman. Ilonka's first
moments of consciousness were disorienting. Her
room was dark and she couldn't see who was
shaking her, if it was even a human being. Also, she
didn't feel as if she were all the way back in her
body. She was still walking beside the Nile, beside
the wise one, under the shadow of the pyramids—
the sun thousands of years younger than the sun she
knew. Instinctively, she slapped aside the hand on
her arm. It was only then that she heard Sandra's
voice.

"Did you hit your mother every morning when
she came to wake you for school?" Sandra asked,
her shadowy form sitting back on the bed away
from Ilonka. She didn't sound angry—Sandra never did.

"My mother never had to wake me," Ilonka said,
her heart racing. "I was always up before her. What
time is it?"

"Almost midnight, time to rock 'n' roll."

25

"No. Really? God, how could I have slept so long?" Then she remembered her mouthful of pills. She sat up and pushed aside the blankets. "Where's Anya? How come she didn't get me up?"

"She told the rest of us that you were sleeping so deeply she didn't want to wake you. But Kevin thought you'd be upset if you missed the meeting."

Ilonka smiled at the thought of Kevin's concern for her. But her smile didn't last long. She reached over and turned on the light. The glare blinded her for a moment. Then she was sitting face to face with Sandra Cross.

It was traditional at Rotterham to define people by the disease they had. At least most of them did, and Ilonka was no exception, although she tried not to. Sandra had Hodgkin's—terminal to be sure, even though she looked relatively well. Indeed, Sandra was the plumpest patient in the whole mansion, which was not to say she was overweight, only not emaciated. Sandra had wavy orange hair that turned red if the light was favorable, hazel eyes that would never pass for green, freckles that didn't miss the sun, and a mouth she was forever trying to stretch with lipstick. She was pleasant, but simple, a member of the Midnight Club only because she wanted to be, not because of the wonderful stories she told. In fact, Sandra had yet to relate a single tale, but she assured everyone that a masterpiece was on its way. Ilonka had her doubts, although she didn't mind Sandra's presence in the group. They needed at least five people present to feel they were talking to a group.

26

"How are you feeling?" Sandra asked.

"Why is it that everybody here always asks everybody else that same question?"

Sandra chuckled. "Because we all look like we need asking."

"You don't." Ilonka squinted at Sandra. "Why not?"

"You ask that as if I've discovered a secret passageway out of here."

Ilonka smiled dreamily. "Wouldn't that be a wonderful story? That there existed a secret door in this place, and if you could find it, and walk through it, you would come out into the real world completely well. Hey, why don't you tell that story?"

Sandra seemed mildly frustrated, which was probably how she felt. "I don't have your imagination, Ilonka. You're the one who should do it."

"No, I think it's yours to tell." A chill touched her right then, out of nowhere, and she reached for her robe. Her window was partway open, that must be it—the night air was creeping in like a breath from the other world. She would have to watch that she didn't catch a cold. Swinging her feet onto the floor, she said, "Let's go. I don't want them starting without us."

Rotterham Hospice offered regular counseling sessions for those who had yet to come to grips with their illnesses. These groups were usually led by Dr. White and were really no more than opportunities for people to unburden themselves, although Dr.

White occasionally did say something useful. Ilonka had attended a couple of them before the formation of the Midnight Club and had felt they were beneficial for those who found comfort in shared sorrow. Yet she didn't feel she fit into that category because she didn't want others to have to take on her sorrow. She wished they could all get up and walk out the door and play baseball, even if it meant they all had to sit on the bench. At least this is what she told Dr. White, who had not argued with her about it.

But the Midnight Club was different. It was about life—sometimes extremely violent life, true —not about death. How had it started? None of them was exactly sure. Spence said it was his idea, but Ilonka thought Kevin had been the first to bring it up. Then again, Kevin said she was the brains behind it. Whatever, the idea had clicked instantly. They would meet in the study at the stroke of midnight. There would be a roaring fire. The stories would flow, they would fly with them, and the nights would be a little less dark. The four of them were already friends: Spence, Kevin, Anya, and Ilonka. Sandra they let come along for the ride. That was it, they all agreed, on one else was to join the club. And the funny thing was, no one else asked to join. The late hour of their meetings may have had something to do with it. Midnight was prohibitive for the deathly ill.

When Dr. White heard of the club, he was enthusiastic, as they knew he would be. But he was surprised when they refused to let him sit in, surprised but not offended. He knew the best therapies were the ones they created for themselves. He offered them the study, the best room in the house, plenty of firewood, and told them to enjoy.

Ilonka and Sandra hurried toward the study, entering as Spence was throwing another log on the already hearty fire. The walls were wood paneled—walnut—the room smelled of wood and old books, no wonder, as the many shelves were stuffed with volumes that could have been brought over with the first American settlers. Ilonka had once found a two-century-old French pornographic novel in the study. At least that was what Spence said it was, who just happened to be walking by at the time, and who just happened to read and speak French. Of course the book might have been about child care for all she knew.

The study was centered on the fireplace, an ancient brick affair that they often joked was big enough to cremate all of them. Although the room was fitted with easy chairs, and even a couple of small couches, they chose to meet at the heavy mahogany table in the center of the room. Here each night they set up silver candle holders borrowed from a cabinet in another room and fitted them with long white candles that burned like holy flames in a medieval church. Ilonka took a seat between Kevin and Spence, and across from Anya and Sandra. Anya was in her wheelchair, as usual, a blue shawl wrapped around her shoulders. A tightness in her features betrayed the fact that she was in pain. Kevin was also wrapped in a blanket; he hadn't changed from that afternoon, except to remove his coat and boots. He continued to be deathly pale. But there was no sense going to Dr. White and asking for a blood transfusion for him because treatment was against the rules. Only painkillers were administered. Ilonka had pain herself, but it was less than during the afternoon, and she suspected the Tylenol was still in her system. She had yet to feel totally awake.

"Sorry I'm late," she said.

"Heard you had a date," Spence said.

Ilonka smiled at the thought. She had never had a date in her life. Her illness had hit when she was fifteen, six months after her mother had died, and she had been in and out of hospitals since. She was the youngest in the group. Her eighteenth birthday was in four weeks. Spence was the oldest, at nineteen. The others were all eighteen.

"Yeah, I couldn't get rid of him," she said. "But I didn't know if he wanted me for my body or my drugs."

"Speaking of which," Anya said, "is anyone carrying? I don't feel so hot."

"You can ask the night nurse," Sandra said.

"I want something now," Anya said. "Spence?"

"I have morphine." He reached in his pocket and withdrew a couple of white one-gram pills. Spence always had extra pain medication on him, though God knew where he got it from because the nurses were strict with what they handed out. He slid the pills across to Anya, who swallowed them with a glass of water. Sandra wore a look of disapproval, but Anya ignored her. The rest of them didn't care one way or the other.

"Let's begin," Anya said.

They all stood up, except for Anya, and hugged each other person, saying, "I belong to you." It was a ritual Ilonka had initiated at their first meeting. It had just come to her—or rather, as she now believed, it had been *given* to her. The effect of greeting each person in this way was dramatic. No matter how isolated they might have felt when they entered the room, before they began their stories they were all one family. Even Anya, hard head that she was, seemed to enjoy each person coming to her and hugging her in her wheelchair. Ilonka hugged Kevin especially hard, and even kissed him on the cheek. She could get away with it at this time.

"I belong to you," she whispered in his ear. He felt so bony in her hands.

"I'll always belong to you, Ilonka," he said with feeling, surprising her. He kissed her in return, on the forehead. The kiss meant a lot to her, like more than the rest of her life that far. It was a shame his lips felt so parched. Morphine did that, and it parched the throat as well. Kevin always sounded dry when he spoke.

She smiled. "Do you mean it?"

His brown eyes were kind. "Sure. Do you have a good story tonight?"

"The best. How about yours?"

"Yours will have to be pretty good to beat mine," he said.

They returned to their seats and turned to Spence. They didn't even ask if he wanted to go first because he always did, and in a way it was good to get the violence over with first, although Anya's inevitable horror was not the best way to finish. Ilonka had decided she was going to try to get Anya to be second. Spence took a sip of some tea he had brought with him. He was at home on stage and Ilonka wished he had had a chance to become an actor, which is what he had been studying before his brain tumor had come a knocking. Like Kevin, Spence was a young man of many talents. Spence set his tea down and cleared his throat.

"This story's called 'Eddie Takes a Step Out,'" Spence said. "It takes place in Paris."

Kevin immediately let out a groan.

"What's the matter?" Spence asked.

"My story starts in Paris," Kevin said. "Put yours somewhere else."

"I can't. I need the Eiffel Tower. You put yours somewhere else."

"I need the Louvre," Kevin said.

"It doesn't matter," Ilonka said. "We're the only ones who'll hear these stories, and I, for one, don't mind if we have two stories set in Paris. I love Paris. My mother went there before she came to America. The people are all rude as hell but the city is the most romantic place on earth."

Kevin stared at her strangely. "I didn't know you had ever been to Paris."

She didn't mind his staring at her. "You didn't notice the international flavor in my character?"

"Hey, everyone can see you've been around, Ilonka," Spence said. "But are we cool on this issue? Two stories in one night that take place in Paris?"

"My story will take more than one night to tell," Kevin said.

"Fine," Spence said with exaggerated patience. "I won't have a Paris story tomorrow night. Now let me begin before anyone else speaks."

Spence had another sip of tea and then started.

"There was this American tourist in Paris named Edward Maloney, or just Eddie for short. He was around forty, a Vietnam vet. His face was badly scarred from the napalm his buddies had accidentally dropped near him while clearing out the jungle. Because of his hideous appearance he had trouble getting girls, unless he paid for them. Even prostitutes didn't like to go to bed with him because it was hard to fake pleasure when they had a monster staring down at them."

"We're off to a great start," Anya muttered.

Spence smiled and continued. "Eddie was in Paris to get a little payback. Most of you probably don't know this, but the French were in Vietnam before the Americans, and in Eddie's mind it was the French who had started the war and been the cause of his misery. Also, like Ilonka said, everyone in town was rude to him since the day he had arrived. Eddie felt he was just going to give back where he felt the giving was due. The night we meet

Eddie he plans to go to the top of the Eiffel Tower with a couple of high-powered telescopic rifles and begin wasting people, one by one. You see, Eddie thinks he can shoot at people for a long time before the police discover where the shots are coming from. His rifles have silencers, sniper scopes, and have a range of over a mile."

"You never have silencers on sniper rifles," Anya said. "Also, you can't shoot with accuracy at over a mile."

"Please, I know more about guns than you. Let me go on. Eddie doesn't want to pull this little caper off alone. He has an old girlfriend from high school who now lives in Paris, which is another reason he has chosen Paris to make his big statement to the world. Her name is Linda, and she left him for a football jock while he was in the army. That was twenty years ago, but Eddie has tracked her down and decided she is to be by his side when he starts shooting. He also plans to use her as a shield when the police finally figure out where the bullets are coming from.

"He goes to her house after midnight. He has a pistol with a silencer as well. He bought all these goodies on the black market in Paris, where, as you might guess, Arab and Israeli arms dealers practically work out of malls. Linda is shacked up with some guy from Colombia, but Eddie has no trouble or compulsion about blowing the guy away."

"Wait," Anya said. "How did he get in the house?"

"No one in Paris locks their doors," Spence said.

"Yeah, they do," Ilonka said.

Spence shrugged. "Well then, he went in through a window. Eddie is a pretty good climber still for an old guy. Anyway, he blows away Linda's boyfriend while the guy is sleeping and jumps on her chest and puts the gun to her head. He said, 'Scream, baby, and it'll be the last sound you hear in this life.' Linda recognized him because she had seen him once after the war. She knows to keep her mouth shut. Eddie told her to get dressed, and then he led her out to his car.

"The Eiffel Tower has got to be the most famous landmark in Paris, but at night when it's closed its security is nothing compared to the Louvre's, or any other famous museum's. That's a fact; it's because you can't steal the tower. You can't do much of anything to it unless you had several cases of dynamite. But it does have some security, and Eddie had to dispatch it so he wouldn't raise an alarm before he got to the top of the blasted thing. But he was lucky in one respect in that he could deal with each level of security individually. If you visit the tower, you start at the bottom, of course, and then you go up a few hundred feet to the second level. Then another few hundred feet to the third level. Finally you enter an elevator that takes you right up the center to the top. Eddie had Linda with him as he parked and walked toward the entrance on the ground floor."

"Can we interrupt if we don't think something is plausible?" Anya asked.

"No," Spence said, insulted. "You're the one who tells stories of demons and witches. How plausible are those? Besides, everything I say is theoretically possible. I've been to the tower. I know guys like Eddie. He's an amazing character, who had this planned for years. Let me continue.

"With one hand he pulled Linda along, in the other he had his silencer pistol. He made Linda carry the suitcase that held the rifles. They were kind of heavy, but he told her if she didn't do her share he'd put a bullet in her brain. She wanted to scream, there were a few people around, but she decided to wait for a better chance to escape.

"At the entrance there were two guards standing around drinking coffee. Eddie didn't hesitate. He shot them both in the chest. Quickly, he hid their bodies. Then he shoved Linda into the elevator that goes up to the second and third levels. It is operated manually, and as they started up, Eddie was feeling good. He was committed.

"On the second level Eddie climbed out with Linda, leaving the suitcase with the rifles inside. He didn't have to stop there—he could have gone up to the third level. But he wanted to knock out all the security in the tower. There were only two security people on the second level. Eddie finished them off in a minute."

"How come Linda hasn't started screaming yet?" Anya wanted to know.

"She's afraid he'll kill her," Spence said. "I've explained that already. Quit interrupting me so then I won't interrupt you. Eddie went up to the third level, where it was the same story: two security guards blown away. Then he transferred Linda and the suitcases to the central elevator and was on his way to the top.

"Here he ran into a problem. There was only one guard at the top, but the guy had been alerted because he had tried to call down to his buddies on the other levels and gotten no response. When Eddie got off the elevator, the security guard ordered him to halt. He was only twenty feet away. Eddie figured the guard wants him to stop—he didn't speak French. And Eddie did halt, for a moment, but then he reached into the elevator and dragged Linda out, holding her in front of him. He put his pistol to her head and said, 'I'll kill her.' But the guard didn't speak English. Besides, he didn't want to lay down his life to save what was obviously an American woman. He took aim and fired.

"The bullet caught Linda above the waist, on the left side, and went right through her. It hit Eddie in about the same spot, only a bit lower. The bullet had lost speed from first hitting Linda and ended up lodged in Eddie's side. They were both seriously wounded, but not bad enough to kill either of them, at least not outright. Eddie fired a return shot and caught the guard in the right eye. The guy went down, dead. Eddie had the Eiffel Tower to himself. But he was bleeding—they both were, pretty bad.

"The top of the Eiffel Tower has both an inside and an outside viewing area. Up there the wind is

37

always blowing—even in the summer it's cold. The door to the inside was locked and Eddie didn't bother taking the dead guard's key to open it. He didn't even bother tying Linda up. She was bleeding enough to keep her in one place, but not enough to shut her up. Not that Linda was a big talker. During all this time, from the moment he blew away her boyfriend, they hadn't had much conversation."

"Yeah," Anya complained. "I'd like some interaction between them before the police blow them away."

"How do you know that's the way it's going to end?" Spence asked.

"You're predictable," Anya said.

Spence rubbed his hands together, getting into it. "I'll give you interaction. While Eddie loaded his rifles he laughed about how he wasted her boyfriend, but Linda just laughed back at him! 'The joke's on you,' she said. 'I've been trying to get rid of that jerk for the last six months. You just did me a favor.' Well, that took Eddie by surprise, but then he saw the humor in it and laughed with her. Linda sat there in her growing pool of blood and told him how ugly she thought he is with half his face burnt."

"Wait a second," Anya said. "I thought she was afraid of him though."

"She is," Spence said smoothly. "But she's losing blood and feeling kind of woozy, almost drunk. Also, she figures that by now she is as good as dead so she may as well get in her licks before he kills her."

Anya nodded, satisfied. "I'd probably do the same. Did her insult hurt Eddie's feelings?"

"Yeah, but he had work to do. His rifles have infrared or sniper scopes on them so he can see as well as if it were daytime. First he scanned across the River Seine to the Avenue des Champs-Elysées, where all the tourists go to shop and gawk at the Arc de Triomphe. There were a few people strolling, although it was now after two in the morning. Eddie focused his telescopic lens on an old man."

"Why an old man?" Anya protested.

"Will you please shut up?" Spence asked. "Eddie can kill who he wants. He took aim at the old man and pulled the trigger. The silencer took care of most of the noise and the wind drowned out the rest. Almost a mile away, the man fell to the ground. A few people ran to see what was wrong. They saw the blood, the bullet wound, and looked anxiously around. Eddie smiled—he felt good, like he was back in Vietnam. Oh, I forgot to tell you—Eddie loved his army tour of duty until they fried his face. For him, Nam was like Disneyland.

"Behind him Linda asked if he has hit someone. He said, 'Yeah, one down, one hundred to go.' Linda swore at him. She was weird but she wasn't a murderer. She had been happy to see her boyfriend buy it, but that didn't mean she wanted to see a bunch of innocents go down. She tried to slow down his slaughter by asking him what he had been doing since they last talked. Like Eddie really wanted to recount his life story to her. After all, she had run off on him with another man and set him on the dark road into madness.

"Yet he did end up talking to her because he had no one else to talk to. But he continued to move around the top of the tower, picking people off, one by one, in different sections of town. Below him he saw the police and ambulances scurrying toward each of his victims. They had no way of knowing where the bullets were coming from—so he thought. He told Linda how he had been unable to find work when he returned home, and how he had had to take drugs to kill the pain in his face, and how he had ended up becoming addicted to the drugs, and how he had started to steal to support his habit. Surprisingly, Linda was sympathetic to him."

"No way!" Anya interrupted.

"I'm not so predictable, am I?" Spence asked, grinning.

"It's easy to be unpredictable when you're incoherent," Anya said.

"All this fits together perfectly," Spence continued. "Let me finish. Eddie had killed maybe thirty people, or at least seriously injured that many, when Linda dropped her bombshell. She said that just before Eddie had gone off to war, he got her pregnant, and that she had the baby, a daughter. Eddie almost fell off the tower at the news. He wanted to know where the girl was, what her name was, why she hadn't told him about her when he came home. Linda only laughed at him. She said, 'Look at you! What kind of father would you have made?' Eddie—you have to grant him this much—could see her point.

"But he still wanted to know about his daughter. He set his rifles down and pulled out his pistol and put it to Linda's temple. It had been easy for Linda to taunt him while he was preoccupied killing others, but having the muzzle pressed into her head scared her. Eddie said, 'Tell me or I'll finish you off right now.' So Linda told him about Janice. She was twenty years old, naturally, and was living in Paris. In fact, she had been asleep in the next room when Eddie broke into her house. That was one of the reasons Linda went so quietly with Eddie, so Janice wouldn't wake up and get killed.

"Eddie was having one hell of a night. On the very day he chose to let the world know how much he hates he finds out he had a daughter. Linda explained that she told Janice her father had died in Vietnam a big hero. Eddie kept shaking his head in disbelief. He finally lowered his gun and said he had to see his daughter before they came for him. Linda said, 'Not until you throw all your guns away.'

"Eddie didn't want to do that. He planned to have a big blow-out with the police before he left the planet. Also, he knew he wouldn't need Linda to find Janice since he had already been to Janice's house. But Linda laughed when he suggested that. 'Janice goes to work real early,' Linda said. 'She'll be gone by the time you get there. Only I can lead you to her.'

"Eddie considered what she was saying. He realized he wouldn't be free long enough to wait for Janice to come home from her job. Suddenly, seeing his daughter interested him more than killing. He picked up his two rifles and pistol and threw them over the side. 'Let's go see her,' he told Linda.

"All this time the two of them had been bleeding and they were both weak. Also, the French police were not as stupid as Eddie figured. They had decided that the assassin terrorizing Paris must be atop the Eiffel Tower. Just as Eddie and Linda prepared to leave, three police helicopters swept in. At the same time our happy couple spotted two dozen uniformed men coming up the tower stairs. The elevator is not the only way to the top. Seeing all this, Eddie pounded his hands on the railing. He had expected to be caught, but he hoped to take plenty of cops with him. Now he had nothing to shoot at them with.

"But there was another gun on top of the tower, the very one that had injured them both. The dead security guard's weapon. Linda hadn't forgotten it. She went for it as Eddie pounded the rails, and now it was her turn to put a steel muzzle to his temple and say, 'Do what I say or I'll waste you.' Linda could see the helicopters approaching. The police barked orders out of them and she waved to the guys. But of course their orders were in French and Linda couldn't understand them because her French was not very good. Eddie began to back away from her as she waved to the cops. Powerful beams of light swept the top of the tower and showed Linda brandishing a weapon and a bloody Eddie backing away from her, afraid. What could they think? They opened fire on Linda and literally blew her head off."

"No!" Anya squealed. "Don't tell me Eddie got away?"

"He was arrested, sure, and held for questioning. But since he wasn't the one holding the gun when the cops showed up they figured Linda was the shooter. The fact that Eddie was wounded substantiated that theory. Also, the Colombian Linda had been hanging out with was a really bad character. They figured the two of them were a gang. They let Eddie go. He returned home to America with his daughter, Janice, who worshipped him because he was supposed to be a big war hero."

"And they lived happily ever after?" Anya grumbled.

Spence shrugged. "No one does that in real life."

"Like your story was true to life," Anya snapped. But then she smiled. "I liked it. I liked Eddie. He was real sick, like some people I know in this place."

"I thought the image of a crazy guy on top of the Eiffel Tower killing people—and no one knowing he was up there—was haunting," Ilonka said. Yet there were many things about the story she thought contrived, like the sudden insertion of the daughter. She suspected Spence had thrown her in as he went along. But she didn't say that because she never criticized the others' stories. She didn't want them criticizing hers. Also, the beauty of a Spence story was its spontaneity. He was always slightly out of control.

"I thought it was kind of violent," Sandra said.

"What do you mean, *kind of?*" Spence asked, not offended. "It was *extremely* violent. I like violence. All of nature is violent. Animals are always killing one another."

"We're not animals," Sandra said.

"I am," Spence said.

"I liked it a lot," Kevin said. "Pure mindless storytelling. It has its place. Who's next?"

"Why don't you go next, Anya?" Ilonka suggested.

"I think it's Sandra's turn," Anya said.

Sandra blushed. "I'm in listening mode tonight."

"Oh, start talking and something will come out," Spence said. "Talk about a terrorist attack. Talk about the return of the Black Plague."

"If Sandra doesn't have a story, that's cool," Kevin said. "Anya, you go ahead. I want to go last, and I know Ilonka wants to go before me so that she's a hard act to follow."

Anya nodded, a bit more relaxed. The drugs were making their way into her bloodstream. She took a sip of water and started.

"This story is titled 'The Devil and Dana.' Dana lived in a small town in Washington called Wasteville, where everybody wasted their lives working and going to school. Dana was blond and delicious but she'd had a strict upbringing and felt that just about everything a girl could do to have fun was sinful. Both her mom and dad were so right wing they were like one-winged birds forever flapping in circles. But Dana had a nasty mind, which tormented her constantly. She wanted to go out with boys. She wanted sex, drugs, and rock 'n' roll. She prayed to God to free her of these base desires, and at the same time she prayed for her desires to be fulfilled. What's God to do with that kind of prayer? The devil came to her instead.

"He walked in just as she was kneeling at the foot of her bed before retiring for the night. You know the devil, he can be a pretty sexy guy when he wants to be, and this night he was dressed in Jimmy Dean's body, tight blue jeans, black leather jacket, and boots. His hair was greasy and he was smoking a cigarette. Dana just looked at him and blinked. She'd never had a vision before. 'Don't worry,' the devil told her. 'I don't bite.' He pointed to her bed. 'Can I sit down? I want to talk.'

"Dana nodded and sat on the bed beside him. Sure, she wanted to know who he was, and he told her. 'I'm the devil,' he said. 'But don't worry, I'm not as bad as people say.'

"Dana didn't know if he was serious or not, but she didn't argue with him, mainly because she thought he was pretty cute. Dana was born way after James Dean was dead and didn't realize she was talking to a clone of sorts. She just said, 'What brings you here?'

"Well, the devil took a drag on his cigarette and

said he had come to make her an offer. 'You want to be a party girl,' he said. 'And you want to be valedictorian. You're like two people in one body and it's not working out. I can help you with your problem. I can make another you, a perfect double. You can be in the two bodies at the same time. You can experience everything your double is experiencing, whether it's sex, drugs, or rock 'n' roll. You can do this even while you're in church praying.'

" 'How can you make another me?' Dana asked.

" 'I'm the devil,' the devil said. 'I can do anything I want.'

" 'Are you really?' Dana asked. About this time she started to really notice him. She realized that no matter how much he puffed on his cigarette it didn't get any shorter.

" 'My talking ain't going to convince you,' the devil said. 'But if you agree to my little bargain, and I make another you, you'll have to be a believer. What do you say?'

"Now Dana became suspicious, because if he was the devil, why would he help her? 'What do you want in return?' she asked.

"The devil smiled, which always had a wonderful effect on women. 'Nothing.'

" 'Nothing? You don't want my soul?'

"The devil waved his hand. 'No. I don't need to win souls. That's propaganda your priests and ministers feed you. Plenty of souls come to me without my doing a blessed thing. No, I'm here to make you an offer with no strings attached. The only thing I ask is that if you enter into this agreement, you have to stay in it for at least a year.'

"Dana was interested. 'Can I extend having a double for another year if I want?'

"'Yes. At the end of one year, if you're satisfied, you can be triplets.'

"His offer sounded good to Dana. She figured she'd go south to L.A., have all the fun she wanted, while her double hung around in Wasteville and did all the things her mom and dad wanted her to do. But there was one thing that bothered her.

"'Won't it get kind of confusing being in two bodies at the same time?' she asked.

"'You have two minds in your body right now. You'll get used to it.' He offered her his free hand, which was devoid of a single line. 'Do we have a deal, Dana?'

"'Don't you need a drop of my blood or something?'

"'No. I have all the blood I need. A simple handshake will do.'

"Dana shook his hand. The devil grinned and put his cigarette out on the floor, which annoyed Dana because she was tidy. Then he stood up and blew out his last lungful of smoke, and lo and behold, it became solid and molded itself into an exact replica of Dana. At that moment Dana felt as if she were in two places at once, which she was. The sensation was disorienting, but cool. Her double stared at her, and she stared at her duplicate because she was in both bodies at once. The devil stood between them and turned from one to the other.

"'Now remember what I said,' he said. 'You've got to be two people for at least a year.'

"'Why do you make that a condition?' both Danas asked at the same moment.

"In response the devil smiled slyly and then vanished.

"Now you might think the two Danas would have had plenty to talk about. But the truth is they didn't have a single thing to say because it would have been like talking to yourself. Yet they did have an argument right away. The double—we'll call her Dana Two—started to leave the house. She had the same idea Dana had had, to go down to L.A. for some heavy partying. The original Dana wanted her double to stay—she wanted to be the one to go to L.A. They fought about it for a few minutes, but then they realized it was an argument neither of them could win. And besides, it didn't matter because even though there were two of them, each could feel what the other felt exactly. So in the end the original Dana let Dana Two go. Dana worried that her parents might notice something odd about the devil's creation, but the truth was even she hadn't noticed any differences.

"The next day Dana woke early, the same time as Dana Two. This was one thing she—or they—noticed right away. Both Danas had to wake up at the same time and go to bed at the same time because the other one would just keep the other up.

It was a pain in the ass but Dana figured it was worth it, what with all the fun she was going to enjoy, vicariously, through the body of her double. At the time Dana Two awoke she was on a bus headed for L.A. Dana had given her double all the money she had—or, rather, her double had taken it. It was the same difference.

"Dana went to school and had a dreadful day because the bus her double was riding was uncomfortable and the trip from Washington to L.A. was a long one. She spent the whole day wishing she could block out what her double was experiencing. But she figured things would pick up when her double got situated. Dana went to bed early that evening because her double was exhausted.

"The next day was better. Dana Two was finally in L.A. and out on the beach, sunbathing in a skimpy bikini. Sitting in class, the original Dana could feel the warmth of the sun on her legs and chest and the grainy sand beneath her butt. I don't know if I mentioned this: Dana was eighteen years old and every schoolboy's dream. She was blond and blue-eyed and had breasts that could have been implants if they hadn't had such bounce to them. It didn't take Dana Two long to catch the eye of the lifeguard. They started talking, and just like that Dana Two had her first date. The original Dana had never gone out with guys. Her parents wouldn't let her.

"Her parents were sitting watching TV beside Dana, a Disney film about furry animals trying to survive a cruel winter, when the lifeguard took Dana Two back to his place for a drink. The lifeguard and Dana Two had already had dinner with wine. You can imagine how hard it was for the original Dana to maintain her composure while she was sitting with her parents. Especially when the lifeguard began to kiss Dana Two real long and real deep and touch her breasts. Dana asked her dad if she could be excused, but her dad shook his head. He was big on the family doing things together.

"So Dana lost her virginity in the same room as her mom and dad, in a manner of speaking. I'd like to be able to say that she was able to keep from crying out when she had an orgasm for the first time, but I'd be lying. Dana let out a real whopper, as did her double, and Dana's mother was so shaken to see her beloved daughter in such a state that she insisted Papa rush Dana to the emergency room. Dana smiled all the way to the hospital, and the doctors could find nothing wrong with her except slightly elevated blood pressure.

"Time went on and life was interesting for Dana. Because Dana Two was really going to town. She didn't stay with the lifeguard long. The guy had a fetish about never wearing a shirt, and when they went out anywhere nice they were always being stared at. She teamed up next with a movie producer who let her stay at his place. This guy—his name was Chuck—had had success with a couple of low-budget movies, but he wasn't a big-time producer by any means. He was still struggling. He told

Dana Two that he saw potential for her on the big screen, and she believed him. They *both* did. Then Chuck turned Dana Two on to Hollywood's favorite low-calorie sweetener: cocaine. Dana Two had a nose for it—if not the brain cells—from the first sniff. She loved the stuff. She would get totally stoned in the middle of the day and the original Dana would sit in class, glassy-eyed, and doodle in her textbooks. Dana began to do poorly in class, but she didn't care because she was going to be a movie star soon. She loved Chuck, too, kind of— he was a fun kind of guy. Sex with him, especially when loaded, was like dying and going to heaven. Secretly, Dana sometimes wondered why the devil didn't just change his name to God and make the whole world a happy place. She felt nothing but gratitude to him.

"But that feeling didn't last because Dana's situation—both of them—changed real quick like. Dana Two came home one day and found Chuck in bed with another guy. He asked her to join them, but Dana Two had been brought up strict and there was only so far a girl could run from her roots. She left Chuck's house and didn't go back.

"Now Dana Two had a problem, and that meant Dana had a problem. Dana Two didn't have any money to support her five-hundred-dollar-a-day coke habit. She began to go through withdrawal and so did Dana, which made it impossible for her to go to school, never mind get good grades. Dana's father was not happy with his daughter's behavior,

51

and he whipped her repeatedly, at the same time that Dana Two wandered the streets of L.A. looking for a place to sleep, food to eat, drugs to snort. It was a miserable life for both girls.

"A few months went by. I could go into more detail about how things steadily went downhill for both of them, but I don't think it's necessary. Suffice it to say that Dana ended up expelled and permanently grounded, and Dana Two ended up homeless and abused. Then, finally, Dana had had enough. She wanted out of the bargain. She prayed to the devil to get rid of her double, but he didn't answer her prayer. Her double had to be aware of her praying and must have told the devil to stay away. Now this might seem a contradiction—that they should want different things. But it's not because, like the devil said, they were like two minds in one body. And in this sense Dana was no different from every teenager. She didn't want *this* because of *that*. *This* was good and *that* was bad. But *that* always preyed on her mind because everybody always wants what is forbidden.

"Dana wasn't praying to the devil or God either now—she was disgusted with God. She thought what an idiot he must be because when he created Adam and Eve in the Garden of Eden he told them that they could have everything they wanted except fruit from the tree of knowledge. Dana thought what a stupid psychologist God must be because, of course, they would want what they couldn't have. Or else God did know what he was doing and was

just playing with them. Either way, God had created the devil and Dana felt she was being manipu-
lated. She decided to take matters into her own
hands because she couldn't stand a year of being
split in two. She would kill her double.

"The instant she made her decision her double
was aware of it, of course. You would expect that
her double would simply flee. But that wouldn't
work because Dana would know where Dana Two
was going. The moment Dana decided the double
had to go, Dana Two decided Dana had to go. They
each blamed the other for their problems, even
though intellectually they understood they were
blaming themselves. But what use are intellectual
thoughts when you feel miserable, huh? They
wanted out of it. One of them had to go.

"Dana's father had a shotgun for hunting. Dana
swiped it and his car and drove south toward L.A.
Dana Two could see her coming and figured she
would wait for her to arrive. But I don't mean Dana
Two waited idly. She got her own gun, a pistol, and tried to work out a strategy. But whatever
she came up with, she saw Dana laughing at her.
They both told the other, telepathically, 'The hell
with it, let's see what happens when we meet.'

"And meet they did, at the end of a crummy
alleyway in one of the worst sections of L.A., late at
night—at midnight, actually. Dana came up the
alley with her shotgun leveled at Dana Two, who
had her pistol aimed at Dana's head. The two of
them moved closer and closer until it seemed one

of them had to shoot. But if one of them was hesitating, the other was as well. They got within ten feet of each other and still no shots were fired.

"'Well,' Dana Two sneered. 'What's the matter? Are you afraid?'

"'If I'm afraid,' Dana said, 'you are, too.'

"Dana Two nodded. 'That's true. But it was your idea to drive down to kill me.'

"'If it was my idea, you gave it to me.'

"'Touché. So at least we recognize that we are blaming each other for our mutual problems. That's a start. How are we going to get to the end?'

"'One of us has to go,' Dana said. 'You know that as well as I do. And since I was here first, I should be the one who gets to stay.'

"'How do you know you're the one who was here first? How do you know where you were standing or sitting when the devil made me or you? He's a crafty devil, you know. Besides, what does it matter? I'm the same as you. I deserve to live as much as you.'

"'You deserve to die as much also,' Dana said, her finger on the trigger of her shotgun. They continued to point their weapons directly at each other. They were both sweating. They were both everything alike, except what they were looking at was not *exactly* the same, even though each was looking at the other. Their perspectives were just a tiny bit different, where they were standing, what they were wearing. It added spice to the drama.

"'Has it occurred to you,' Dana Two asked, 'that if you kill me you might be killing the fun part of what you are? That maybe the devil did split us slightly, and that if I'm gone all the fun will go out of your life?'

" 'Has it occurred to you that if you kill me you might be killing all the good in your life?' Dana asked.

" 'No,' Dana Two said. 'And it hasn't occurred to you either, because you don't feel anything good living at home with those two loons.'

" 'That's true,' Dana admitted. She thought for a moment. 'So what are we going to do? We're not going to make it through a whole year the way things are going.'

" 'I agree.'

" 'One of us should let the other shoot the other,' Dana said.

" 'I agree. I'll shoot you.'

" 'How about I shoot you?' Dana said.

" 'How about we both shoot at the same time?' Dana Two said.

" 'Then we both might die,' Dana said.

" 'But we're going to do that anyway. Because the moment you shoot, I'll shoot. And vice versa.'

" 'But maybe that's what the devil wanted,' Dana said. 'Maybe he foresaw all this. If we both die he will have won and we'll probably end up in hell together.'

" 'That's a good point,' replied Dana Two. 'But we won't know until we try it.'

" 'I have a shotgun,' Dana said. 'You only have a pistol. You will need a lucky shot to kill me.'

" 'My pistol's a forty-five,' Dana Two said. 'I

55

don't have to be that lucky.' She paused. 'Come on, we're both going to shoot and we both know it. Let's do it. Let's shoot on the count of three. But let's not cheat because that's the least we can do for each other. Do you agree?'

" 'Yeah,' Dana said. 'One.'

" 'Two,' Dana Two said.

Anya stopped talking and took a sip of water. A long sip.

"Well?" Spence said finally. "Don't tell us you don't know what happens next."

"I do know," Anya said reluctantly, her face oddly serious.

"Tell us, for God's sake," Ilonka said, totally enthralled.

Anya allowed a faint smile. "Since this is a story about deals with the devil, Ilonka, I find your choice of words ironic. But let me tell you what happened. They both shot at the count of two. They both tried to get the drop on the other. One of them was killed, the other seriously wounded, crippled for the rest of her life. It's a sad story, I know. For the rest of her days one of the Danas was confined to a wheelchair. Then, toward the end of those days, the devil came to her again, still looking like James Dean. He had a fresh cigarette, though, and he asked if she would like to make another bargain with him. At first she said no because of what had happened the first time, but the devil persisted. He said, 'If you make this bargain with me you'll never experience hell.'

"That caught her attention. She asked what she had to do.

" 'Kill yourself,' the devil said. He gestured to her ruined body. 'Just kill yourself and this hell will end for you. You should have killed yourself a long time ago.'

" 'But what about my soul?' she asked.

"The devil shook his head. 'Only God knows about that.'

" 'Is that true?' she asked.

" 'Have I ever lied to you before?' the devil asked.

"She thought a moment. 'I suppose not. But what you're saying is that you don't know.'

" 'I don't know,' the devil agreed. 'To tell you an even bigger truth, I don't even know if there is a God. It's one of those mysteries that's hard to figure out.' He stopped. 'Which one are you, anyway, Dana Two or the original one?'

"Dana shook her head. 'I can't remember any-more.'

"The devil nodded. 'Good luck to you, Dana.'

"Then he vanished."

Anya stopped and had more water. She made them wait. Finally she looked around, apparently enjoying her brief moment of power over them, and laughed. "That's it, fellas, the story ends there."

Spence protested. "You can't do that to us."

"Honestly, I don't know what happens next."

"Make something up," Spence said.

Anya held his eye a long moment, her seriousness

57

returning. "I don't just make things up, Spence. You know that."

Spence became quiet. "Well," he said. "It had a hell of a start."

"It was a killer all the way through," Kevin said enthusiastically.

"I liked it," Sandra said.

"If it was a book I'd buy two copies," Ilonka said.

"Hey, how come you didn't offer to buy my story?" Spence asked.

"Yours was more the kind you check out of the library," Ilonka said.

"Or else borrow from a friend," Kevin said, joining in the fun.

"If you were real bored," Anya added. She paused and suddenly blushed. She spoke softly. "Thank you for listening to me and not interrupting. I really wanted you all to hear this story. It seemed to have a lot of things in it that I—I don't know."

"What?" Ilonka asked.

"It's nothing," Anya said, shifting in her wheelchair, probably the same kind of chair Dana ended up in at the end. "You're up, Ilonka. What's the title of your story?"

Ilonka had not considered that. "It doesn't have a title."

"Make one up," Spence said.

"I can't."

"Why not?" Spence asked.

Ilonka hesitated. "It's a story from one of my past lives."

The room became still and deathly quiet. Spence was smiling, as was Anya. Sandra looked confused. Only Kevin was watching her closely, studying her.

"Do you remember past lives?" Kevin asked.

Ilonka had to take a breath. She realized she was trembling, probably from embarrassment. She hadn't meant to say the story was from her past. It just slipped out of her mouth.

"I don't know," she said. "I think so."

"Are any of us in this past life?" Kevin asked.

Ilonka stared into his brown eyes, as warm and welcoming as a fire on a winter prairie, and she believed beyond a shadow of a doubt that she had seen them before two weeks earlier. Yet it was odd at that moment that she should lie to him.

"No," she said. "There's just me."

Kevin continued to study her, his cheek bones high, his skin as smooth and pale as a vampire's. "Interesting," he said. "Tell us your tale."

"It was in Egypt twenty-thousand six-hundred and fifty years ago," Ilonka began. "I know that's about thirteen thousand years before we think ancient Egypt existed, but that's how it comes to me. At that time there were pyramids close to the Nile. But the Nile was not where it is now, but six miles to the east. Anyway, these details are not important, and if you don't believe them I don't mind.

"My name was Delius. As the story starts I was about twenty-seven years old, tall and thin, very austere. I was not married, but there was a man in my life, a very great man. He was my Master. I don't remember his name. I think that's because I always called him 'Master.' He was like Jesus or Buddha or Krishna. He was filled with the divine. Near him, the feeling of love, of power, and most of all, of *presence* was profound. He had many supernatural gifts. He could heal, know what any person was thinking and be in more than one place at the same time. But these gifts were not what made him great. It was how he could change a man or a woman's heart that was the true miracle. Being around him, people became like him. They became divine. That's why he was on earth: to bring people back to God. I loved him a great deal and always felt like I would do anything for him.

"I had a friend at the time, a very special friend named Shradha, who had a thirteen-year-old daughter I was close to. That was Mage, darling Mage. Shradha and I were so close I felt as if her daughter was mine. But even though Shradha loved me, she was jealous of my relationship with her daughter. Mage would listen to everything I said, and she looked up to me as if I were her teacher. But with her own mother, Mage was often stubborn. You know how irritating our own moms can be. It was the same long ago.

"Once I invited Mage to my house to spend a few days. Mage was delighted, but Shradha had doubts. She didn't like her daughter away from home because the times were dangerous. There had been a drought for many years, and food was scarce. People act crazy when they're hungry and do things they would never ordinarily do. Shradha and I got into a fight over Mage coming to my house, and Mage saw and heard the whole thing. When I left, still thinking Mage would be visiting, Mage told her mom that she was going to a friend's house. Shradha tried to stop her, but Mage ran out the door and was gone.

"Later—it was later that same afternoon, I believe—I returned to fetch Mage but found no one at home. I decided to pack Mage's things and carry them home so she wouldn't have the burden of carrying them. Years before I had made a bag for Mage out of coarse linen. On the outside of the bag I had stitched Mage's name. If I close my eyes, I can see the symbols now, like hieroglyphs, but simpler. I placed everything I thought Mage would need in the bag and hiked back to my house, which was four miles away.

"But unknown to me, Mage was dead. While hiking to her friend's house the young girl had been ambushed by two starving men. This will be difficult to hear—it's painful for me to even think about—but they killed Mage so that they could eat her. In the latter years of the drought cannibalism was common. Mage's remains were found by a local peasant and her identification was made possible by a scarf she wore. But there was not enough left to bury. Certainly not enough left to prepare in the ways the Egyptians at that time liked to prepare the bodies of their dearly departed. While I was at Shradha's house, Shradha was being led by a peasant—a man who had worked for the family—to her daughter's bloody remains.

"Shradha returned home totally devastated. But something she saw there lifted her spirits. Mage's personal items were gone. Shradha believed her daughter's spirit had come for the items before leaving for the next world. You see, they believed the spirit had a use for such things even dead. That's why personal items were buried with the dead. That was part of the religion of the time, but it was not one of the teachings of the Master. Very few followed the Master in those days because he had predicted that the drought would not last, but it went on for seven years. He had made a false prediction on purpose so that only his devoted followers would stay with him. Throughout eternity the Master would first appear as godlike, and then appear fallible. But he would always be the same eternal being inside.

"Shradha's only comfort in the days immediately after her daughter's death was that the girl had come home to take her things. Eventually she had a chance to see the Master and told him what had happened to her daughter. And he said, 'Yes, I know, I was with her when she died. You need not worry. She is fine—I took her into the light.'

"At these words Shradha was happy, and she said, 'Yes. I know her spirit still lives. She came home for her things before she left.' But the Master told her the truth. 'No,' he said. 'That was Delius who took Mage's things.' When he saw Shradha's shock, he added, 'But she did not do so to deceive you. At the time she did not know that Mage was dead.'

"Now what happened next was as sad as Mage's death. Because even though the Master had assured Shradha that I had not meant to hurt her, Shradha could not help feeling devastated by the news. In the midst of her pain, the only thing she had had to cling to, that gave her hope her daughter was still alive somewhere, was the missing personal items. And now it turned out it was just a foolish act on my part. Also, at the back of her mind, Shradha felt that if I hadn't insisted Mage come to my home, they wouldn't have had the argument and Mage wouldn't have run out of the house.

"I understood all these things, when I was told what had happened. I tried to assure Shradha that I had meant no harm, but our friendship was never the same after that, which was a great waste be-cause we could have given each other great comfort. Before Mage's death, even though we occasionally argued, we were as close as two people could be. But when Mage died, the light in Shradha's life died and she could not be reasoned with.

"There is a bittersweet ending to this tale. I did not live long after that. I died of heart failure when I was only thirty-nine. I was aware the end was near for the Master had told me how long I was to live. A week before I passed on I met with Shradha and told her again that I had meant no harm when I took Mage's things. And Shradha could see in my eyes my sincerity, and she hugged me and promised that when we met again, we would never allow 'misunderstanding to come between us.'"

Ilonka suddenly stopped talking and lowered her head. Her eyes were wet and she didn't want the others to see. She especially didn't want to look at Kevin—at Shradha—at that moment. If she turned her head in Kevin's direction Shradha was there. But it was Kevin who reached over and touched her arm.

"Are you all right?" he asked.

She sniffed and raised her head, forcing a smile. "I don't know—I feel stupid. It's just a story, you know. It doesn't mean anything."

"It was a beautiful story," Kevin said. "Did you ever meet Shradha in this life?"

Ilonka sighed, clasping her hands together. "If I did she was still mad at me."

"I don't believe in past lives," Anya said. "But I loved your story."

Sandra was sniffling, too. "It was so sweet," she whispered.

"I think it could have used more description in the cannibalism scene," Spence said. "But otherwise it was nice. What did this Master teach, by the way?"

Ilonka shook her head. "I can't explain now. So many things, yet only one thing. To be what we were, to be God. But in those days we used to say, 'I belong to you.' That's where I got the idea for it. The Master always stressed how we were all one."

"You feel you really knew him," Spence said.

Ilonka shook her head slightly. "It could all just be imagination but I feel it was a past life. Thank you for your compliments—really—I was scared to tell the story. Only with you could I share it." She turned to Kevin. His hand was still on her arm, so tenderly. Wiping her face, she grinned at him. "So, am I a tough act to follow or what?"

He let go of her. "Always," he said. He had a glass of water as well, and he took a drink before he began. Sometimes he had to stop a story in the middle because his throat would give out. He was so frail, her Kevin, and that was not her imagination.

"My story is called 'The Magic Mirror.' It starts in the Louvre in Paris. For those of you who don't know the museum, it is probably the most famous in the world. The Mona Lisa and the Venus de Milo are there, as well as many other great paintings and sculptures. To see everything inside would take several days.

"As the story starts we meet a young woman about Ilonka's age named Teresa. She is from—I'm not sure where, not America, Europe, but not France. Since I mentioned Ilonka, let's say Teresa is Polish. Teresa is visiting Paris alone and like most visitors goes to the Louvre. Right away she notices the artists who work at the Louvre copying the paintings of great masters of the past. On any given day at the Louvre, there might be twenty or thirty artists at work copying. Some are students, many are quite accomplished artists. Most are extremely good. But there is one artist in particular who catches her attention. He is copying da Vinci's *The Virgin of the Rocks,* which depicts Mary with the infants Christ and John the Baptist in the care of an angel. They are sitting in the shadow of a grotto. A mysterious vista, which gives the illusion of the dawn of time, extends behind the grotto. The painting, although not da Vinci's most famous, is one of the most significant in Western art, and my personal favorite. The angel in particular has a beautiful radiance—it is as if da Vinci caught her soul with his paints. It is a painting you can stare at for hours and see something new each minute.

"Teresa is intrigued by the painting, and even more so by the artist who is copying it. Because his painting seems to be every bit as good as da Vinci's. Also, he is a striking young man, not much older than herself, and at the time Teresa was very lonely. Like I said, she came to Paris by herself, but this was because she was an orphan. She strikes up a conversation with the artist and learns his name is Herme. But she's not sure if Herme is French because he doesn't have a French accent. In fact, she can't place his accent and asks him where he is from. But Herme evades the question.

"Herme has a good reason for not telling her where he is from. If he did she would think he was crazy. You see, Herme is not a human being, but an angel. He is a particular angel we would call a 'muse.' I believe it was the ancient Greeks who invented the term. A muse inspires our great writers, painters, poets, and musicians. Herme had been da Vinci's muse when the artist was alive, and also Raphael's and Michelangelo's. In a sense their creations were his. But in this modern age there is no artist capable of tuning into Herme's inspiration, and so he passed his days copying at the Louvre. He could only work on the physical plane, appear as a human being and paint, while he was at the museum. If he left the Louvre, he was just like any other angel, and people wouldn't know he was there. But it was a thrill for Herme to be seen by humans, to be able to talk and ask questions. God had given him this special opportunity because of the great work he had done in the past.

"In the same way Teresa liked Herme, he liked her. Her face intrigued him—he had an artist's eye for faces. Her eyes were warm and gentle, her mouth touched with sadness. Her voice, also, intrigued him because Teresa could sound like an innocent child and a wise woman in the same sentence. She was beautiful, and he was so taken by her that he suggested they have lunch together in a museum café, an invitation which Teresa readily accepted.

"Herme put aside his paints and his canvas and walked with her down the museum's long halls, pointing out various paintings and telling her stories about the artists, personal things like how van

Gogh cut off his ear and gave it to a prostitute or how Michelangelo didn't really like to paint but only wanted to sculpt. He told her other things that even the experts wouldn't know about the artists. Teresa was fascinated by his knowledge and his soft manner. I guess it goes without saying that Herme was nicer than your average person. It was his love that shone in many of the works of the artists he had helped. He was also attractive by human standards, with long brown hair, an austere face, and big fine hands. But his clothes were simple: white pants and a blue shirt. He wore no watch, or anything like that. He didn't have a wallet, for that matter, and when they reached the snack bar and picked up their food, he was embarrassed. He had to apologize that he had no money. But she didn't mind paying for the food, even though she had little money of her own.

"So they talked and ate and Herme learned a great deal about Teresa, although Teresa learned almost nothing about Herme except that he was a great artist and knew art history like a scholar. Teresa was sensitive and knew somehow that Herme was like no human being she had ever met. By the time lunch was through, she was in love with him, and Herme, being an angel, could see into her heart and knew her love was genuine. And for him it was special because even though he lived in the constant glow of God's love, a secret part of him craved human affection. He had worked with humans for so many centuries that a part of him had become human. Maybe more than a part. When it was time for Teresa to leave the Louvre, he felt lonely. She promised to come see him the next day.

"At noon the next day, there she was, as Herme was putting the final touches on his copy of *The Virgin of the Rocks*. Teresa couldn't get over how talented he was, and she went so far as to say his painting was better than da Vinci's. But Herme quickly corrected her that it only looked better because his paints were fresh. In reality Herme never tried to surpass the works of the artists he had helped, although privately he thought that he could. They ate lunch together again, and once more Teresa paid, which made Herme feel uncomfortable because he wanted to take care of Teresa. She told him of her plans to go to America and dropped not-so-subtle hints about how much money he could make in America with his talent. Her enthusiasm was infectious and Herme had to stop to remind himself that he wasn't flesh and blood. That reality hit him painfully when Teresa asked him to go with her to see a movie. He told her he had to stay to finish his work, but Teresa, stubborn at times, tried hard to talk him into it, which only made him feel worse. He finally had to give her a firm no, which she misinterpreted, thinking that he didn't care for her. Just before she left, he asked if she would come to see him the next day, and she promised she would.

"The following afternoon went much the same as the previous two, except their feelings for each other were more intense. Once more Teresa wanted Herme to leave the museum with her. But he said he couldn't, not until later. She wanted to know how much later—she was willing to come back for him. When he said that would not be possible, she began to suspect that he had another woman or that he was married. But he assured her that was not the case, even without her having voiced her suspicion. That caught her off guard, that he seemed capable of reading her mind, but he quickly smoothed over his comment as a coincidence.

"Poor Teresa didn't know what to think. She had met this wonderful guy but he seemed unnaturally attached to a museum. He wouldn't tell her where he lived, how he got to work, if he had any other family. Really, when she thought about it, she realized he had told her nothing about himself, only about the artists whose paintings hung in the great halls. Herme could read her mind and he knew he couldn't have her come back day after day to see him. He realized that he was going to lose her, and that brought him more pain than he had ever known, the first real pain he had ever experienced. He made her promise that she would visit him the next day, and this she did, but there was a reluctance in her voice. The fact of Herme asking for her promise—his asking for anything—was very unlike him. Because he was an angel, and angels simply gave, and asked for nothing in return.

"That night, alone in the Louvre, Herme prayed to God to allow him to leave the museum and go out with Teresa. He prayed for many hours, and then, suddenly, he felt a great warmth enter his soul, and he knew that God had granted his prayer. But simultaneously he realized that when he left the museum he would never return to it as an angel. He would become entirely human and lose his angelic powers. But this he was willing to do for the love of his Teresa. I say *his* Teresa and that's what I mean. Already he believed he would have Teresa with him for the rest of the life he had chosen.

"The next day she came for him, and Herme left the Louvre. He walked outside into bright sunlight, Teresa's hand in his, and laughed out loud. He was so happy, so much in love. He thought it would last forever, but of course he had never been mortal before."

Kevin stopped talking and reached for his glass of water. They waited anxiously for him to continue, but he shook his head. "That's all for tonight, folks. I'm sorry."

"Do you know the rest of the story?" Anya asked.

"Yes," he said. "But I want to tell it in parts. I can't think up a new story every night. I want to get full mileage out of this one."

Ilonka didn't believe him for Kevin was the most creative one in the group. He was probably trying to keep them in suspense. She did worry, however, that he might have stopped when he did because he was tired. His voice had begun to weaken toward the end. She clapped softly in approval.

"It's a wonderful story," Ilonka said. "I'm like Teresa, I'm in love with Herme already."

He lowered his head. "You are a lot like Teresa, you know. You're both Polish."

She laughed. "You added that at the last second." She almost added that he couldn't have chosen a better name if he *had* wanted to pattern Teresa after her because her middle name was Teresa. But she knew no one at the hospice knew that, not even Dr. White, since she never used her middle name. She didn't want to give Kevin the impression that *she* thought he would put her in one of his stories, oh no, not that, even though she was telling him stories of their past lives together.

"I think it's a wonderful story, too," Sandra said. "I can't wait to see how it turns out."

"I'll reserve my judgment for the time being," Spence said. "Many a story can start out great and then fade. I've had it happen myself a few times."

"You've had more start awful and then get worse," Anya told him. She shifted in her wheelchair, absently smoothing her hand over a spot just below the stump of her leg. Ilonka had often seen her make the movement before, as if she were trying to rub a spot on her leg that no longer existed. "There's been a lot of talk tonight about God and angels and devils and past lives. Does anyone here *really* think that we survive after death?"

"Are you trying to spoil the festive mood or what?" Spence asked.

Anya's anger flared. "No. I'm asking a serious question and I'd like to know your opinions. What is it?"

"I have no opinion," Spence said.

Anya continued to be annoyed with him. "You must have thought about it, seeing where we are."

"I have thought about it," Spence said. "That's why I have no opinion. I think it's the only honest opinion to have."

"I believe in God," Sandra said. "I believe there's a heaven and hell."

Anya smiled wickedly. "Which one do you believe you will go to in the next few days or weeks, Sandra dear?"

Sandra gulped. "Heaven, I hope. I've always tried to be good."

Anya chuckled. "If that's the main criteria for getting into heaven I don't know if I want to go there." She scanned the room. "How about you, Kevin?"

"I believe in the soul. I think the experiences of people who've had near-death experiences strongly points toward the idea that something survives the death of our bodies. I don't believe in heaven or hell in the traditional sense of the words. If there is a God, I can't see why he would create a place to torture people for eternity just because they made a few mistakes on earth." Kevin paused. "But I also believe that my beliefs don't matter much. What is—is. I can't change a thing. Do you know what I mean?"

"I don't," Ilonka said, watching him closely. She

had never heard Kevin speak so openly before, about anything. Ordinarily she had to grab glimpses of his feelings from his stories. He looked over at her and shook his head.

"Maybe I'm as bad as Spence," he said. "I only know that I don't know."

"How about you, Ilonka?" Anya asked. "Or need I bother asking you after your past-life story?"

Ilonka was thoughtful. "I don't know about having a soul. Sometimes I'm sure I must have one. Other times I feel there's nothing inside. But I do believe that love survives. That the love we feel in our lives doesn't vanish. That God keeps track of it, saves it so that it is always there, more and more love in the universe. Then maybe each time we come back there is a little more love waiting for us."

"If we do come back," Anya said.

Ilonka shrugged. "I won't know until I do."

Spence sat up. "But that's why these discussions are a waste of time. We won't know what it's like to die until we die. Maybe the bright light people who've had near-death experiences see will turn out to be nothing more than the brain's last attempt to stave off the horror of nonexistence." He paused. "It's a pity that the first one of us to go can't come back and tell the others what it's like."

Sandra made a face. "That's an awful thought."

Spence wore a strange expression, as if, even though it was his own idea, it shocked him. "What's awful about it?" he asked. "I think it's the best idea this club has ever had."

Ilonka laughed uneasily. "I don't want any ghosts knocking on my door in the middle of the night."

"But what if it were a ghost you knew?" Spence asked. He addressed the whole group. "I'm serious about this. Why don't we take a vow that the first one of us to die is to make every effort to contact the rest of us? What do you think, Kevin?"

"You are suggesting that the one in question give us a sign?" Kevin asked.

"Yes," Spence said.

"Do you want us all to agree upon a prearranged sign?" Kevin asked.

"No," Spence said.

"But if the sign is random, how will we know it's from the dead person?" Kevin asked.

"The sign could be anything," Spence said. "We could meet late at night as usual and our dearly departed could knock over a lamp or something."

"It might not be possible, as a ghost, to do something so dramatic," Kevin said.

"Let's stop talking about this," Sandra said. "I don't like talking about it."

"It's intriguing," Anya admitted.

Sandra was outraged. "When people die, they don't hang around the earth and give people signs. It just isn't done."

"If it isn't done, then it doesn't have to scare you," Spence argued.

"I am not scared," Sandra said indignantly. "I just think it's unnatural. Ilonka, say something."

"Could the person who dies communicate with us telepathically?" Ilonka suggested, warming to the possibility. She realized that when she got right down to it she was as curious as anybody else. Spence shook his head.

"That would be too abstract," Spence said. "We would never know for sure if we didn't imagine it."

"But what if the dead person made us all dream the same dream?" Ilonka asked. "That would be proof, of sorts."

"That's an interesting idea," Kevin agreed. "Assuming someone on the other side can influence our dreams. How about if we use a Ouija board and try to contact the person?"

"We could ask Dr. White to buy us one," Spence said, interested.

Sandra shook her head. "I will not agree to this. If I die I'm going straight to heaven, and that's the end of it."

"Don't worry," Anya said. "If you're the first one to die none of us will be in a hurry to talk to you."

"Now, now, be nice," Spence said. "Sandra, I didn't ask for a contract, you don't have to sign anything. But if you don't want to do it, that's fine. But think how you could put the rest of us at ease if we see that you're still kicking on the other side."

"You're assuming it will be a relief to know that we do have souls," Anya said.

"You really are in a bad mood tonight," Sandra told Anya.

"It's my natural state," Anya said sweetly. "That's why I'm not anxious to make it eternal."

"I think the first of us who dies will have to

decide on the other side the best way to contact the others," Spence said.

"That may be true, but we should give him or her some idea of where we will be looking for a sign," Kevin said. "But we can think about that later."

"Not too much later," Anya said. "You never know in a place like this."

"Are we all agreed then?" Spence asked. "Sandra?"

"As long as I don't get in trouble with God I guess it will be all right to try," Sandra said, doing an about-face.

"I'm for it," Kevin said.

"Me, too," Ilonka said.

"We should take a blood oath," Anya said. "It will add power to our intent."

"I don't think that's necessary," Spence said.

"I don't mind taking a blood oath." Ilonka said. "It will add a pagan flavor to our vow."

"It doesn't exactly matter if we catch anything from each other," Kevin said.

"Somebody get a needle," Anya said. "We'll smear it altogether and chant our vow in unison."

Spence was shaking his head. "Let's not turn this into a sideshow. We all agree to try our best to contact the others. That's all that matters."

"But we want the blood ceremony," Anya said.

"You can have it if you want," Spence said, standing up. "I'm going to bed." He turned toward the door. "Good night, everybody. Sweet dreams. No one die during the night."

"He left all of a sudden," Ilonka said when Spence was gone. She didn't feel tired herself, probably because she had slept half the day away. Kevin was beginning to nod in the chair beside her, his messy brown hair hanging over his bony face. She touched his arm. "Hey, sleepyhead, you have to get to bed."

Kevin raised his head, his face brightening. "Why don't you give me an escort?"

She felt herself blush. "I should probably take Anya back to our room."

"I can get back to the room without your help," Anya said. "Sandra can help me."

"As long as you don't bite my hand," Sandra said, getting to her feet and stepping behind Anya's wheelchair. Anya had cancer in her right arm as well as her remaining leg and didn't have the strength to push her wheelchair. Dr. White was trying to get her a motorized chair but it was going to take time he said—and would probably be too late when it did arrive. Sandra and Anya left the room on a chorus of good nights and Ilonka was left alone with Kevin.

"I guess we're not having a blood ceremony," she said.

"I guess not," Kevin said. "What did you think of Spence's suggestion?"

"I thought perhaps he might have been up to some scheme to make us all look foolish," Ilonka said. "Until he said that someone might fake the sign. That's what I thought he might do. But I think it's an interesting idea."

"Yeah."

"I really did love your story," she said.

Kevin had a faraway look in his eyes. "Thank you."

"How was your visit with Kathy?" she asked.

"Fine."

"She seems like a nice girl. How long have you been going together?"

"On and off for the last two years."

"Why sometimes off?" she asked.

He glanced at her. "I've been in the hospital a lot."

"Of course, silly me."

He shook his head. "I just wish I had told her at the beginning that I was sick. I knew, you know, I just thought I'd get better. The doctors did, too."

"Maybe you will," Ilonka said.

He smiled, but his face remained sad. "I'm not counting on it."

"Why were you looking for me today?"

"I heard you're going to get a scan tomorrow."

"Who told you that?"

"Dr. White. Don't be upset with him, he just confirmed what I had heard. You must have told someone."

"I did tell Anya. She must have told Spence."

"I'm sure that's the way it went," Kevin said. "Anyway, I was just wondering why you're going for the scan. But if you don't want to talk about it, I don't mind. It's none of my business."

"Did Dr. White ask you to talk to me?" Ilonka asked.

"No."

She shrugged. "I've been feeling better is all, and I think the tumors are shrinking. You know, I've been taking a lot of herbs and eating a really pure diet, just fruits and vegetables."

"I didn't know that," Kevin said.

"Look, if you're worried I'm getting my hopes up for no reason, just tell me."

"Only you know how you feel."

"That's what I told Dr. White."

"So there's no problem. Get the scan, and if you're cured be sure to write."

She wanted to tell him that she couldn't imagine leaving the hospice without him. But what was the point? He still looked like he was going to pass out. She stood up and grabbed him by the arm, something she had never done before.

"If you don't go to bed now you'll still be here tomorrow night for our next meeting," she said as she helped him to his feet. Once more his thinness hit her, his lightness; it was as if she were helping up a sack filled with feathers. He leaned on her for support.

"So you really never met anyone that reminded you of Shradha?" he asked.

She almost told him right then that she had been talking about him. But she couldn't, and really it was stupid given their circumstances. Was she so proud? She had never thought of herself that way before.

"No," she said. "I told you no."

"When you were talking about Egypt I felt as if I was there."

"Yeah? Interesting."

She led him to his room. He hugged her before he opened the door, and it was nice to be held. The nicest thing in the whole world. Then he abruptly said good night and was gone. She walked back to her room with a special bounce in her step.

As she fell asleep, she thought she saw the Master's face and knew she would dream of him.

─ Chapter III ─

THE MORNING WAS COLD AND DAMP AS ILONKA PAWLUK and Dr. White drove toward Menlow General where Ilonka was to have her test. Dr. White's car was plush but Ilonka found it uncomfortable to be traveling. Her sleep had been fitful, and she had ended up taking two Tylenol 3 tablets at four in the morning. She had taken another two after her breakfast of an orange and an apple, just before Dr. White had come for her. Her abdomen was one huge hot cramp. She didn't know why she was having so much pain all of a sudden. Dr. White noticed her discomfort.

"We'll be there in twenty minutes," he said.

She nodded. "I'm fine."

"Did your club meet last night?"

"Yes. The stories were particularly good. Spence only mutilated a few bodies and Anya's devil wasn't half as bad as we all expected him to be. Kevin told a wonderful tale about an angel who falls in love with a girl and then becomes human so

82

that he can be with her. He didn't finish it, though. He's supposed to tell us more tonight."

"What did Sandra talk about?" Dr. White asked.

"Sandra hasn't told a single story yet."

"What was yours about?"

"Some people in ancient Egypt." She felt a sharp stab of pain in her guts and sucked in a breath. "It's hard to describe in a few words," she whispered.

"Ilonka?"

"I'm all right." She forced a smile. "Tell me about your daughter. Jessie?"

"Yes. That was her name."

Ilonka froze. "She's not— No."

Dr. White was thoughtful. "It may have been a mistake to bring her up the other day. But I've wanted to tell you about her. It was Jessie who inspired my work with young people like you, and you, more than anyone, remind me of her. When she was growing up I used to think she was just stubborn. But at the end I saw how valiant her spirit was." He shook his head sadly. "She died of cancer two weeks after her eighteenth birthday."

"It's my eighteenth next month," Ilonka said stiffly.

"I'm sorry, I shouldn't have—"

"I'm glad you told me about her," Ilonka interrupted. She touched the doctor's arm. "Really, it's all right. Tell me more about her. Tell me what her favorite music was, whether she had a boyfriend or not. Tell me whatever you want."

Dr. White did as she requested, slowly at first, in

halting sentences, then more openly. Before they'd reached the hospital Ilonka learned that Jessie White had loved many of the same things Ilonka loved—a good book; the Beatles; science-fiction movies; trees; boys, of course boys. Jessie had had a boyfriend when she died, Dr. White said, someone to comfort her. Ilonka found it both a joy and a burden to hear about the dead girl. Her pain, even with the pills she had taken, continued to mount. She never imagined a car ride could be so hard on her. She had to wonder at her own stubbornness.

Ilonka found the hospital overwhelming after the quiet of the hospice. Naturally, when they tried to check in for the magnetic resonance scan they learned there was no record of an Ilonka Pawluk in their books. While Dr. White hurried off to pull some strings, Ilonka was left sitting in a hard green plastic chair not far from a door that kept opening and closing to the outside, the gusts of cold air cutting her like scalpels. One gust was so strong it knocked her wig slightly askew, and she was horrified until she hastily fixed it. She sat with one hand on her head and the other hugging her bottle of Tylenol and codeine, telling herself she wasn't going to take any more pills and at the same time wondering how she was going to be able to lie still for the hour the scan lasted. In the end, just before they finally called her in, she swallowed another two pills. For the first time in a long time she wished she had morphine.

In the test she had to lie in a long coffinlike

machine. The magnetic resonance technique did not use X rays to see inside the body but computer-controlled sound waves. These waves built up a "picture" of the various densities of her internal organs. A tumor generally showed up as a shadow in this picture because of its high density. While lying in the chamber, listening to the eerie hum of the electronic eyes as they slowly revolved around her, she remembered the first time the test had been done and the dismal results. They had operated on her the very next day, and when she had awakened they told her she no longer had a uterus or ovaries. Just like that she learned she was never going to have children. She had wept at the news and had hardly heard them say they weren't sure they had gotten all the cancer.

Ilonka suddenly felt a terrible longing to see her mother, whom she told everyone had died of cancer but who had really drunk herself to death.

The longing remained with her throughout the test.

Dr. White was in a quiet mood on the way back. The people at the hospital had told the two of them they would have the results by the next day. Without the stimulus of conversation Ilonka found her head frequently falling, and she was angry at herself for having taken so many painkillers. The drugs would just depress her immune system, she thought, and she needed it at peak efficiency to kill the tumors.

Dr. White had another appointment and

dropped her at the front door of the hospice. She thanked him for taking her for the test and hurried inside.

Sitting in the waiting room was Kathy Anderson, Kevin's girlfriend. She stood up as Ilonka went into the room. She had more expensive clothes on, and she flashed a big toothy smile that Ilonka found distasteful. The girl appeared far from comfortable.

"I'm waiting for Kevin," Kathy said. "I've been waiting awhile."

"I'll get him for you," Ilonka said automatically, turning for the door that led into the hospice. But then she stopped—something stopped her. She glanced back at Kathy. "Kevin is very sick. It might be a good idea if you didn't take him outside today."

Kathy shrugged uneasily. "We don't have to go outside."

Ilonka took a step toward her. "Kathy— May I call you 'Kathy'?"

"I don't know what else you'd call me."

Ilonka smiled, but there was no warmth in it. She thought, just before she started speaking, that she was doing Kevin a favor. Yet even with the rationalization came the thought of Judas, the way his mind must have worked. Yes, Jesus, don't mind these soldiers come here to arrest you. They'll take you straight to Pontius Pilot and you can work a few miracles and the guy will love you, I'm sure of it. Then we'll be on our way to Rome.

Yet she went ahead and opened her mouth.

Because Kevin belonged to her. Any fool could see that.

"Kathy, do you realize how sick Kevin is?" Ilonka asked.

The blond girl blinked. "I know what he has. I'm not stupid."

"I'm not saying you're stupid. I'm saying you're carrying around a big case of denial. Kevin has leukemia. With the drugs that are available today, a lot of leukemia is curable. But for some reason the drugs didn't work on Kevin. That's why he's here. This is not a *hospital*, where patients hope to get better. This is a *hospice*, where patients are made comfortable until they die."

A shadow crossed Kathy's face. "What are you trying to say?"

"I have already said it. Kevin is not going to get better. He is not going to leave here some day with you. He is going to die."

Kathy shook her head hard. "No."

"Yes." Ilonka took another step toward her, till they were practically touching. "He is probably going to die soon. And it's hard for him, as he approaches the end, to play this role with you. To play that he's going to get better. In fact, each time you come to see him it hurts him."

Kathy lowered her head and began to cry. "I don't want to hurt him. I love him."

Ilonka put her hand on the girl's shoulder. "Then let him go. Let him die in peace without having to pretend for you. Leave him to us."

Kathy suddenly jerked her head up. Her entire demeanor had changed. She shook off Ilonka's hand as if it were a spider crawling on her shoulder. "And what will *you* do for him?" she asked bitterly.

Ilonka met her glare. "I will stay with him when he dies so that he doesn't die alone. Do you really think that you could be with him at that time?"

Kathy continued to regard her with loathing. Suddenly she turned and ran out of the hospice, slamming the door behind her. Ilonka stared at the same door for a long time afterward, asking herself what she had done, and why.

Finally she heard someone at her back. She knew who it was without turning.

"Ilonka, have you seen Kathy?" Kevin asked. "I heard she was waiting to see me."

Ilonka sniffed. The cold had gotten her nose running, or else it was something else. Yet she looked Kevin right in the eye and shook her head.

"I haven't seen her," she said.

Ilonka went to her room. There she found Anya asleep in a pile of pillows and blankets. The Bible lay open on the floor near her. Anya had a box of personal items sitting on top of her nightstand. Ilonka fell onto her own bed, facedown, and cried into her pillow. She couldn't remember when she had ever done anything so low. She couldn't remember when she had ever wanted someone so much in her life. The two, she knew, bore a definite connection.

After some time she heard Anya call her name. She sat up and glanced at her roommate, who was reaching for a bottle of pills and a glass of water. Of course, once more it was the nurses who were supposed to be handing out the medication, but Anya never played by the rules, especially not this late in the game.

"What's wrong?" Anya asked. "Or is that a stupid question?"

Ilonka sat up. Incredibly, considering how many pills she had taken, her abdomen was killing her. "What are those?" she asked.

"Morphine. One gram each. Want one?"

"I have never taken morphine."

"Once you take it, nothing else satisfies."

"That's what I've heard. That's why I haven't taken it." Ilonka paused and wiped away the sweat that was creeping into her eyes. She was having trouble breathing, she hurt so much. She stuck out her hand. "Give me one," she said.

Anya tossed her a pill. Ilonka had a glass of water by her bed. The pill went down smooth. "How long before it takes effect?" she asked.

"Pretty fast," Anya said. "You'll begin to feel some relief in fifteen minutes."

Ilonka sighed. "I never wanted to be a junkie."

"There are worse ways to die."

"Are there?"

Anya raised an eyebrow, shifting uncomfortably in her bed. "What happened? Did Kevin tell you he couldn't make a long-term commitment?"

"Not quite. I told his girlfriend that she was making a mistake thinking about the long term with him."

Anya was interested. "Tell me the whole story."

Ilonka did, which didn't take long. When she thought about it, she had hit Kathy hard and fast. Anya nodded her approval.

"You did the girl a favor," she said. "Better to face reality."

Ilonka was doubtful. "I didn't say what I did as a favor to her. I did it to keep her away from Kevin." She began to cry again. "It's like I'm so pathetic I can't get him on my own. I've got to wreck his relationship with his girlfriend first."

"You do have a point there."

"Thanks a lot. You don't have to agree with me."

Anya started to speak but then thought better of it. She rubbed at the place her leg would have been, as she often did when she wasn't feeling well. Then she reached over into her box of things and withdrew a small orange clay sculpture of a guy and girl holding hands. The sculpture was broken; it was a curious coincidence that the girl's right leg was the only thing missing. Anya held it up and studied it as if it contained great secrets.

"I made this," she said finally.

"I didn't know you sculpted." The statue had remarkable detail, given its size, and looked to be the work of a skilled artist. Anya continued to stare at her broken work.

"I made it for a friend of mine," she said.

Ilonka caught something in her voice. "For your boyfriend?"

Anya swallowed heavily, and Ilonka thought she

caught a trace of dampness in her eyes. And Anya, so people said, had not even wept when they cut off her leg.

"Yes," Anya said. "His name was Bill. I never told you about him, did I?"

"No."

"Well, there's nothing to tell."

Ilonka moved to her bed, sat down. "Anya. Tell me. You are my friend, you know. I feel that way."

Anya chuckled and shook her head. "You have lousy taste in friends." She tapped the bed lightly with the sculpture. "Hell, it's not even that long a story. I couldn't tell it at our meetings, that's for sure." She paused. "Do you really want to hear about Bill?"

"I do."

Anya took a breath. "Like I said, he was my boyfriend. I met him when I was sixteen, two years ago. I met him at the mall in the bookstore. I've always been a sucker for a guy who reads—there are so few of them. When I first saw him, I thought he looked funny. His hair was a weird orange color, and he wore an earing that looked as if it had been swiped from an African native. He was in the real-life murder section. He had about three of those kinds of books in his hands, so I knew right away I was dealing with a disturbed mind. I was sitting on the floor reading a book of poetry and I remember the way he looked over at me. He just smiled like he knew me, like here he was and there I was. He walked right over and asked me out. Of course I told him where to stick it, but he didn't mind and we kept talking and eventually I gave him my number.

"That was the beginning. Soon we were dating regularly, something I had never done before. Oh, yeah, I had gone out with lots of guys but never one I felt something real for. But there was just something about Bill—I can't explain it. It was like that ritual you started at the beginning of our club meetings, like he belonged to me and I belonged to him. He wasn't the weird person I thought at the beginning. He was a lot more stable than me. He was just fascinated by detective work and stuff like that. In fact, even though he looked like a criminal, he wanted to be a cop some day. He had plans, Bill did, and when he talked about them I was always a part of them."

Anya fell silent for a moment before continuing. "I don't know why the hell I did it. I was happy with Bill. I didn't want to go out with anybody else. But I began to feel, as the months went by, that I was too happy with him. I know that sounds stupid—it is stupid. But it was like he was too nice to me, you know, like I didn't deserve him. Even when I was in his arms, loving him with every cell in my body, I felt like a part of me was betraying him. And this was before I even did anything. It was like deep in my soul I knew it couldn't last because of who I was. Does that make sense?"

"Yes," Ilonka said.

Anya shrugged. "Somebody else asked me out. I can't remember where I met him—I can't even remember his name. Oh, yeah, it was Charlie. Charlie asked me out and I said all right—the words just came out of my mouth. Because I didn't want to go out with him. He was obviously trouble from the word *go*. Then again, I had always been attracted to trouble, until I met Bill. But what I did was go out with Charlie the same night I was supposed to go out with Bill. And I didn't even call Bill to tell him I wasn't going to be available. I just shined him on, you know, I was such a bitch.

"But that isn't the half of it. It isn't a billionth of it. You see, my parents were away for the weekend and I went ahead and invited Charlie back to my place, knowing it would only lead to us having sex. I also knew for a fact that Bill would not be at my house waiting for me. Bill didn't know my parents were out of town and he never got near them. They didn't like him—they didn't like any guy I saw. Boy, I thought as I let Charlie in the front door, what they would have thought about my latest date! Charlie was the kind of guy who was so slimy you felt like you had to spray your hands with disinfectant after touching him. But there I was, ready to screw my brains out with him. Don't ask me why, Ilonka, there is no answer except that I'm a fool.

"So it happened. We were in the house maybe five minutes and he pinned me up against the wall and started kissing me like I was a piece of plasterboard he was trying to drill a hole into. Ten minutes tops and we were naked and in bed. The weird thing was—the whole time—I hated it. I kept wishing I was with Bill. Right in the middle of the act, I closed my eyes and tried to pretend as hard as I could that it was Bill. I prayed to God it was him."

Anya stopped and closed her eyes.

"Bill walked in?" Ilonka said gently.

Anya nodded, a tear slipping out of her right eye.

"Bad timing," Ilonka whispered.

Anya opened her eyes and snorted. "The timing was my own. I see now, in some perverted way, that I wanted it all to happen as it did. If I had just wanted to go to bed with Charlie I could have gone to his place. And I said there was no way Bill was coming over to my house, but you know it was always there—the possibility—since I hadn't called him. That's another thing: I wasn't surprised when the light suddenly went on. It was like a part of me had been waiting for it.

"Bill walked in and there we were, the two of us, blinking at Bill. He stared at me right then, and what hurt the most was not that he looked simply mad. That was to be expected. But he stared at me as if he didn't know me. That hurt the most because of what I said earlier. The day we met, it was as if we had known each other a thousand years. Kind of like your past-life stories. But that night, when Bill saw me, I could have been a worm he had thought was long dead."

Anya stopped and held up her clay statue. "I was making this for Bill when this happened. As you can see, I still had to paint it. It was supposed to be the two of us—I was going to give it to him for Valentine's Day, which was the next week. I had it on my chest of drawers, near the door, when Bill walked in. After giving us his long hard stare, he reached over and grabbed it and threw it to the floor. He was just reaching for something to break. But that was all he did. He didn't try to hurt either of us. He didn't even say anything. He broke this statue and then he turned around and left. I never saw him again."

Anya stopped once more. She had no more tears, but the pain on her face went deeper than her illness. Ilonka leaned over and hugged her, and Anya buried her face in her chest. They sat there like that for a minute. Then Anya whispered something Ilonka didn't catch and she had to ask her to repeat it. Anya pulled away.

"I said the only part he broke was my right leg," Anya said.

"On this statue? Yeah, but that doesn't mean anything. Anya, you don't think you got cancer in your leg because of what happened that night?"

"I got sick a year after that, in my right leg. I got sick and they cut it off."

"But that was a coincidence. You know how these diseases run. You probably had the cancer for years before you knew it."

"Maybe," Anya said.

"There's no 'maybe' about it. Look, you did something that you feel guilty about. That's bad, yes, it makes you feel bad. But it's not why you got sick."

Anya touched the broken leg of the girl on the clay statue. "There's being sick in the body, and there's being sick in the soul." She shrugged. "It doesn't matter. Like I said last night, we probably don't even have one."

"You said you haven't seen Bill since. Does he know you're here?"

"No. I thought of writing him but there didn't seem any point."

"What did you want to say to him?"

Anya's lower lip trembled. "That I was sorry."

"You should write him. You should call him."

Anya put the statue back in the box. "There isn't time."

Anya didn't want to talk about it anymore. Ilonka returned to her bed and lay down beneath the covers. The morphine in her bloodstream chased after her, and she was too tired to run from it. Soon she was asleep. Soon she was awake only in her dreams.

It was another time. Maybe another world. But what was time and space when everything was one? That was what the Master said. What is reality? Who are you? All this that you see, all this that you know with your senses, is maya—illusion. You are beyond that. You are supreme.

She was going to see the Master now and was trying to remember the many things he had told her before. But his words were like those of a whispered poem: intoxicating to the ears, so soft and subtle, but difficult to comprehend, at least with the mind. He said he did not speak to the mind, only to the heart. It was unfortunate her heart was so filled with sorrow—that she could not hear better. Ah, well, he understood that. He understood everything about her, and still he loved her.

She found the Master sitting beside a gently flowing river. His hair and beard were long and dark, his eyes large and lustrous. He smiled as she approached and that was enough to ease her burden, that he should see her again and remember her. She had not seen him in two years, and in that time she had lost everything she loved. He bid her sit beside him.

His was a gentle peace—it almost seemed as if the wind could stir and sweep it away, like a single petal of a flower on a breeze. Yet she sensed that beneath his delicate quiet was the power that moved the entire universe. He did not speak at first, just looked at her, and she found her eyes moist.

"You traveled far?" he asked finally.

She nodded. "Yes, Master."

He played with a rose in his hand. "Your husband is not with you."

"No."

"Ah," he said. "That is it. He is gone and you feel lost."

Fresh tears sprang to her eyes. "I am lost. He left me and he's not coming back. I don't know what to do. I can't stop thinking about him."

"You can't stop thinking about him," the Master agreed. "What you resist persists in the mind. It is always that way. So you are thinking about him. Observe that. Wonder at it. Even the enlightened have emotions. But whereas you act on them, they just wonder at them." The Master laughed and

tapped her lightly on the head with the rose. "It is a wonder that you are here."

She had to laugh, even though she cried. "Will he come back to me some day?"

The Master shrugged. "I don't know. If he does, he does. If he doesn't—that, too, is inevitable. But you don't need his love."

"But I do! His love meant more to me than anything in the world!"

The Master shook his head. "No, you don't need it. You are love."

She nodded. "I understand that intellectually. It just doesn't help me right now." She touched the hem of his robe. "Please bring him back to me."

"Ah." The Master was thoughtful. "What would you do if I brought him back? Would you love him better? Or would you just love him because of what he could do for you? What he gives to you?"

"I would love him unconditionally." She replied like that because the Master always emphasized that they had been born to learn unconditional love. But he laughed at her answer.

"You can love him unconditionally now. You don't need to see him. The only reason you want to see him is so you can get something from him." The Master shook his head. "I have seen you go through this more times than you remember. When you are with him it is all feverish. You become so entangled, so attached. Is it any wonder the universe should take him from you? No, you don't need him. You have me, you have God. It is enough that we love you."

She had been counting on a magical wave of the hand from this Master, who had raised others from the dead with just such a wave. But he would not help her, and she didn't understand why. Once more, though, he read her mind.

"I see that all this pain is good for you," he said. "It turns you back to your inner self. You do not have to be so emotionally needy. Close your eyes and be still. Learn to enjoy your own company." He tapped her on the head once again with his rose. "Go now. Rest."

She was shocked at the sudden dismissal. "But I am still so hurt."

"Emotions come and go—your hurt cannot last. You give such importance to your emotions. I don't know why."

She stood up reluctantly. "Will I see him again?"

The Master closed his eyes briefly. "Yes."

"In this life?"

But that question he would not answer.

CHAPTER IV

IT WAS TIME FOR ANOTHER MEETING OF THE MIDNIGHT Club.

Spence had brought two bottles of wine and six glasses.

"We must have a toast," he said as he passed out the glasses. They had just finished doing "I belong to you."

"What's the occasion?" Ilonka asked.

"Today is the first day of the rest of our lives," Spence said and quietly laughed at himself and his cliché.

Tonight is the start of the endless night.

Ilonka glanced around, wondering where her thought had come from. She quickly dismissed this as ridiculous since all her thoughts originated inside her own mind. But the sentence could have popped into her head from an outside source, it felt so alien. She searched the faces of those in the room and her eyes came to rest on Anya, who sat in pain and exhaustion. Ilonka had slept for a couple of hours after Anya's tale of Bill, but after awakening she had been unable to coax Anya to talk further about the matter. Ilonka was contemplating finding Bill and putting the two of them in touch. Anya could scream at her all she wanted, Ilonka didn't care.

"That it is." Ilonka agreed with Spence. She had never tasted wine before and was looking forward to it. Her own pain was far less than earlier. She was feeling optimistic that her test results would show her tumors were shrinking. That wouldn't mean she was well—she wasn't that foolish—but it would mean she *could* get well. That was all she wanted, a second chance.

Vaguely she remembered dreaming of her Master, and that had also made her feel better. Yet—it was very odd—in the dream she hadn't agreed with what he told her. She couldn't imagine arguing with a being like that.

"Where did you get the wine?" Kevin asked. It was difficult for Ilonka to even look his way, for a variety of reasons. There was her guilt over what she had told Kathy and her fear that Kathy might have called him and told him what the cruel and evil Ilonka Pawluk had told her. There was also Kevin's dreadful appearance—his cheeks were so hollow he could have been the austere angel he spoke about in his story. That evening Spence had had to help him to the study.

Sandra—she looked as she always did, not bad.

"I got it by ordering it through the mail," Spence replied. "They didn't even ask for my fake ID, which I would have been happy to supply. It's a wonderful world we live in when you can buy sin and degradation in a catalog." He finished passing out the glasses and reached for one of his wine bottles. "I say we kill this bottle before we begin our stories."

"I just want a sip," Sandra said.

"You will take your medicine like a grown woman and not complain," Spence said. "You must have a full glass. Who knows? It might loosen your tongue and we could hear a story from you tonight."

Spence walked around the table, pouring the wine as if he were a waiter. When he got to Ilonka's glass, he frowned and picked it up. "Sorry, my Polish Princess," he said, studying the crystal, which he had no doubt borrowed from one of the many cabinets in the mansion. "I believe this one is a little dusty. Fortunately, I was wise enough to bring an extra glass." He pulled out his spare and poured her an ample portion. The dark red fluid looked like blood in the haze of the candlelight. A moment later they were all seated and Spence was proposing a toast. He raised his glass high and they did likewise.

"To the Midnight Club," he said. "May the wonder of its creative genius inspire many to take up the dark and dangerous, and always erotic, path of late-night storytelling. Cheers!"

"Cheers!" everyone said. They couldn't all reach to clink their glasses, spread out as they were around the wide wooden table, but Ilonka was able to clink with Kevin. He smiled at her as they did so and she didn't detect even a trace of resentment in his eyes.

Yet the wine was a disappointment for Ilonka. She had imagined it would taste like glorified grape juice sprinkled with nectar. Instead she found it quite bitter and wondered if that was the alcohol in it. The others, though—probably all experienced wine drinkers—seemed happy with the stuff. In fact, *Sandra* asked for a second glass, which Spence was only too happy to give her. One bottle down, one to go.

Finally they settled down to tell their stories. Spence wanted Anya to go first because he said he wanted to follow her and blow her ass out of the water with his great tale. But she said she had no story to tell.

"But surely the devil must have visited someone else between last night and now?" Ilonka asked, prodding her. Anya shifted uncomfortably in her chair, rubbing her fingers together repeatedly as if they were suffering from arthritis. Her face was so pinched with pain it was as if she were an old and wrinkled woman.

"The devil is always one step ahead of me," Anya said. "I don't know what he did between then and now. I have no story for tonight." She glanced at Ilonka. "I said what I have to say."

Ilonka realized she was referring to that afternoon. She had already told her story for the day. Kevin spoke up.

"You're just working on a big story to blow us all away," he said.

Anya smiled faintly. "Yeah."

"Sandra," Spence said. "Feeling talkative yet?"

Sandra had already finished her second glass, and there was a glint in her eye as if—yes, she was drunk. Just two glasses of wine. Sandra had a wild smile on her face, which suited her better than her blunt haircut.

"I feel like talking about the first boy who ever made love to me," Sandra said suddenly, slurring her words. Spence howled and the rest of them chuckled. Sandra shoved her glass at Spence. "Give me another sip."

Spence had the second bottle open in a moment and soon, further fortified, Sandra was ready to officially join the club. Her grin was as big as her face.

"His name was Dan," Sandra said. "I met him in a park in Portland. I was feeding the ducks and he was there with his dog. His dog didn't like the ducks. It tried to eat a couple. It actually caught one and ripped out a mouthful of feathers. Anyway, I met Dan and we got to talking, and then we went into the woods and had sex. It was my first time and it was great." Sandra burst out laughing. "That's my story."

They all stared at their prim and proper Sandra. Ilonka finally broke the silence. "That's it?" she asked. "You'd known the guy a few minutes and you had sex with him?"

Sandra was suddenly indignant. "We talked for a couple of hours." Then she cackled again. "We talked about sex!"

"Wait a second," Spence said. "What was it about Dan that was so special that you set aside your conservative background and jumped his bones?"

Sandra was obviously puzzled. "I don't know. He wasn't that good-looking. It must have been the wine we were drinking."

Spence cleared his throat. "Enough said." He glanced around at the rest of them. "I guess I should start, unless someone else wants to go first? No? OK, but before I begin I wanted to say I got another letter from Caroline today, and she may be coming for a visit in two weeks. Before that time I'm going to need some things from the pharmacy that the nurses aren't passing out, if you know what I mean."

"You're so sick I'm sure you're sterile, if not impotent at the same time," Anya said. "You don't need condoms."

"I assure you that a tumor in the big head has not affected the little head in the slightest," Spence said. "Ilonka, I heard you're going out tomorrow. Can you stop at the drugstore on the way back?"

"It was today I went out," she said, surprised Spence should have forgotten that fact, he had such a good mind for details.

"Oh, that's right, never mind then," Spence said, quickly dropping the issue. "Let's get on to my story. This one's called 'Sidney Burns Down His School.'"

"We should assume Sidney is related to Eddie from last night?" Ilonka asked.

"Distant cousins," Spence said. "Sid is still in high school as the story starts. He's a senior and never been out with a girl. He's introverted, but an expert magician who occasionally puts on small shows for his friends. He likes this girl named Mary, and he shows her a few of his tricks, at lunch at school, and she tells him how fabulous he is. Her words give him confidence and he asks her out, and she says yes. On the date he shows her more of his tricks and she convinces him that he must put on a show for the whole school. Sid has his doubts, but Mary's enthusiasm wins him over. She promises him that they can even make him money on the deal, besides making him one of the most popular guys at school. Sid has always wanted to be popular.

"Mary had been really popular at school, but lost it. The year before she was a cheerleader and had every guy in school asking her out. But at the end of the year she was at a party and got real drunk. Driving home in her father's huge semi, she smashed into a car holding six guys from the football team—including the quarterback—and wasted them all."

"Wait a second," Ilonka said. "Her father loaned her his semi to go to a party?"

"Exactly," Spence said. "He knew about his daughter's drinking. He figured if she crashed into something in his semi she wouldn't get hurt. And she didn't get a scratch, although she did destroy the heart of the football team. Of course the next year the team did dreadfully and everyone blamed

Mary. They wouldn't even let her be a cheerleader anymore. So by the time Mary hooked up with Sid she was feeling pretty resentful.

"Sid, of course, knew about Mary's past, but he didn't know she hated the entire student body. So he went along with her plan to put on a big magic show. Mary was to be his assistant. You know how magicians are always sawing girls in half and stuff like that. Sid needed a girl to spice up his act, and Mary volunteered to work with him every day after school. You can imagine the wonders that did for Sid's ego. By the time the big day arrived, Sid was feeling invincible.

"But the show was a disaster. Sid planned to start by levitating Mary ten feet into the air. But unknown to him, Mary wanted Sid to fail and she sabotaged the trick."

"But why?" Anya interrupted.

"Listen," Spence said. "Mary was only a foot or two in the air when she suddenly fell onto a foam mat that had been set up below her. But that wasn't the end of Sid's magic show, although more than a few people in the audience laughed at him. His next few tricks went splendidly, but these didn't involve Mary. Just when he was getting the audience back on his side, he did a trick where he had to transfer Mary from one stand-up box to another. Well, of course, Mary didn't move—she was still in the original box. This time the audience laughed hard. Sid's confidence was shot. He did the next couple of tricks by himself, but he was so badly shaken that he flubbed them. When it came time for Mary to return to help him, the audience was hooting and howling at everything he did. But Sid knew he could redeem himself if he could just pull off his grand finale, which involved burning Mary to ashes and reconstructing her and having her suddenly appear on the top row of the gymnasium bleachers.

"He set everything up perfectly. He got the fires going under the pot that Mary was in. When he put on the lid, everyone gasped and wondered how Mary could be in such a hot pot. They gasped again a few minutes later when Sid removed the lid and there was nothing inside except a pile of ashes. But then, when Sid snapped his fingers to have her reappear, nothing happened. Unknown to him Mary had taken the opportunity to walk out on him. Naturally the school exploded in laughter and boos. In fact, people actually started throwing papers at Sid. He left the gymnasium in total disgrace.

"Surprisingly, Sid wasn't even sure Mary had betrayed him, especially when she told him that she had got stuck and that the equipment had failed and so on. To be sure Sid was gullible when it came to a pretty face. But one thing Sid knew for certain was that he wanted to get back at the school for laughing at him. Mary didn't actively encourage him to seek revenge, but in her own subtle way she dropped hints that the student body certainly did deserve to feel his wrath. Sid started planning—what was the worst possible thing he could do to them? Then he came up with an idea. It was horrible, brilliant, something only Sid could dream up. You see, from the time Mary had started to talk to Sid, she realized he was one guy who could really sock it to the school. She had led him by the nose to this moment, to this decision, and he didn't know it."

"If she was smart enough to lead him that far," Anya asked, "how come she couldn't have thought up her own plan?"

"The truly clever always use others to do their dirty work," Spence said smoothly. "Just look at the crooks in D.C. Anyway, Sid decided to burn down the gym during a basketball game, when everyone was inside. Being a magician, he was naturally a master at picking locks. The night of the big game, he stole into a oil refinery and made off with a gasoline truck whose tank was chock full of fuel. He reached the gym toward the end of the second half and drove his truck right up to one of the back doors. Then he quietly went around and chained each of the gym doors shut. Oh, did I mention that this was one of those old-style gymnasiums with a single row of tiny, metal-reinforced windows completely out of reach? You've seen the kind. They're up thirty feet on the wall. I think half the ones in the country have this kind. Sid had them locked inside nice and tight.

"Now it was time for the fun part. Sid had a drill and he punched a six-inch hole into the metal door in the far corner. The noise inside the gymnasium was so loud no one noticed a thing. But that same noise dropped to a whisper when Sid got the hose from the tank and began to pump a torrent of gasoline over the wooden gym floor. Yeah, I think it would be safe to say the game came to an abrupt halt.

"Then the screams started. The smell of gasoline is unmistakable, and probably everyone inside realized that if there was a madman out there psychotic enough to pump in gasoline, he would be crazy enough to set it on fire. Everyone rushed for the doors. The screams grew louder because the doors wouldn't open. People piled on top of one another, smothering themselves in a mountain of flesh. Watching through the same hole he was using to pump in the gasoline, Sid suddenly felt regret. He wasn't a bad guy at heart, he had just been so humiliated he had got carried away. But now that he saw people getting hurt, he wanted to stop. He pulled his hose out of the hole in the door before his gasoline truck was completely empty. He was trying to figure out how he could get the doors open and let everyone out without getting into trouble, when something hard and heavy struck him on the back of the head. Sid went down in a blur of stars and pain. Through the blood dripping into his eyes, he saw a figure put the hose back into the hole in the door and restart the gasoline pumping. He tried to sit up. The figure turned and laughed at him. It was Mary.

"'I knew you would come up with something brilliant,' she said. 'But I also thought you would chicken out at the last minute.'

"'Mary,' he mumbled. 'Why?'

"'They have it coming,' she said.

"Sid tried to stand up to stop her but he was too dizzy and fell back to the ground. He watched helplessly as Mary finished pumping in the gasoline and then tossed aside the hose. She drew a lighter from one pocket, a rolled-up newspaper from the other.

"'Don't!' Sid pleaded.

"'Don't worry, I won't tell the police about your stealing the gasoline truck.' She lit the newspaper and waved it before Sid's eyes. 'And I suppose you won't be telling anybody about me.'

"'I'll tell them everything,' Sid swore.

"Mary knelt by his side, holding her flaming paper near his face. 'I hope you don't mean that,' she said. 'Because if you do I'll have to kill you now.' She leaned over and kissed his forehead. 'I kind of like you, Sid, even if you are a nerd.'

"'I'm not a nerd,' Sid said angrily. His head was beginning to clear, bit by tiny bit.

"Mary laughed. 'Yes you are. But you're a sexy nerd, and I never had one of those before.' She pressed the flames practically in his hair. 'What's it going to be, darling?'

"'I won't say anything if you keep working with me in my magic show,' Sid said.

"'Deal,' Mary said. She stood up and shoved the flaming paper through the hole in the door. The screaming inside suddenly got a lot louder, so loud it literally shook the walls of the building. 'One thousand die-hard fans,' Mary marveled out loud. She helped Sid away from the gym and back to her car as the pitiful cries slowly began to fade and the building began to collapse. In the distance, Mary and Sid could hear the approaching fire trucks. But they were long gone before anyone else arrived."

Spence stopped talking and took a drink of wine.

"Is that it?" Ilonka asked. "They got away with it?"

"Not exactly," Spence said. "A year later Sid was doing a magic show in a club on the other side of town. He had begun to work regularly with Mary after getting out of high school. Their relationship was fine as far as the sex went—Mary could have sex six times a day and still feel deprived—but Mary was always getting on Sid's nerves with her constant need to be in control. She'd taunt him that she could turn him in to the police at any time, that no one would believe a cute ex-cheerleader like her had torched the entire student body. She just didn't understand that there was more to Sid than met the eye. One evening at the club he had Mary in that special box that magicians use when they supposedly saw people in half. Only this time he had fixed the box so that Mary's body was trapped lengthwise. As the blade cut into her, she began to scream, but, of course, the audience thought it was part of the show. Even when the blood began to drip onto the floor the crowd didn't know there was a problem. Sid pulled the box apart, and the two sides of Mary were exposed, two bloody sides. By that time Mary had stopped screaming."

Spence halted again.

"Did he get away with the murder?" Ilonka asked.

"Sure," Spence said. "He just told the police he didn't know what went wrong, he had successfully done the trick dozens of times before. Sid eventually went on to headline a major magic show in Las Vegas. I believe he's there to this day." Spence paused and smiled. "That's my story for the night."

"I thought it was pretty hot," Ilonka said. "No pun intended."

"I liked the idea of the people trapped in the gym with the gasoline pouring in," Kevin said. "It reminded me of your Eiffel Tower story in that each uses one single powerful image. You're a natural to write for the movies, Spence."

"Thanks," Spence said, pleased. Ilonka knew that he especially looked for Kevin's approval, since Kevin was clearly the most intelligent one in the group.

"All the people in the gym just died?" Sandra asked. "That's kind of gross."

"*Gross* is my middle name," Spence said proudly. He glanced at Anya. "Any comments?"

Anya was in obvious pain and withdrawn. "No," she said.

Spence seemed troubled by her remark. "At least tell me if you liked it or not," he said.

"I'm sorry, I spaced out and stopped listening," Anya said, which was probably the most insulting thing she could have told him. The one rule of the Midnight Club was that each storyteller was granted the undivided attention of the others. But Spence didn't appear so insulted as he did nervous. Yet he said nothing more.

Kevin wanted to go last, so Ilonka was up next. She started off by telling them that she had another past-life story.

"It takes place in ancient India," she said. "I don't know how long ago, but well before recorded history. My name at the time was Padma, which means lotus flower. But I won't start the story with myself, but with my mother before I was born. Her name was Parvati, which was one of the many names for the great Goddess. When Parvati was about sixteen years old she met a man named Visnu, and immediately fell in love with him, and he with her. Unfortunately for the two young lovers, they were not from the same caste. Parvati was a Brahmin, the highest caste, which was assigned to priests, and Visnu was a Sudra, which was the laboring caste. At that time it was forbidden for people to marry between castes. It is hard to imagine how strict this rule was followed, but even today in certain parts of India people can't even conceive of marrying someone outside their caste. The union of a Sudra and a Brahmin was particularly prohibited—like putting the highest and the lowest together.

"Parvati and Visnu knew they were meant to be together, but they were afraid to run away to try to start a life elsewhere. They also didn't want to hurt their families. Finally they decided they simply couldn't see each other anymore. Visnu left the area, and a proper husband was arranged for Parvati. Arranged marriages were the norm in those days.

"The night before her wedding, Parvati was in deep distress. She had met her husband-to-be, and although he was a fine man she knew she would never feel for him a tenth what she had felt for Visnu. Before going to bed, she knelt and prayed to the great God Shiva to take her from this world of misery. Her health wasn't good and she knew it wouldn't take much to push her over the edge. She prayed for a long time and didn't stop until she heard a sound outside her window. There was a pack of four dogs gathered around the fountain in her family's courtyard, drinking the water. She didn't understand how the dogs could have got inside the courtyard since it was kept locked at night. She hurried outside to see if a gate had been left open and it was then she saw the *siddha* sitting by the water, the dogs licking his hands. 'Siddha' is a Sanskrit word for a perfect being, a saintlike person, an enlightened yogi. Parvati knew she was in the presence of someone great because of the wonderful feeling of love and power that emanated from the man. The siddha bid the dogs sit quietly and gestured for her to come close. Parvati wondered if it was not Shiva himself who had come to her, since it was well known that Shiva liked to roam the earth in the company of dogs. With her palms folded in a prayerful gesture, she knelt at the feet of the siddha. He removed a yellow jewel from the folds of his robe and handed it to her. He spoke softly.

"'This jewel is a symbol of your love for the one

you think you have lost,' he said. 'It is also a symbol of his love for you. While that love lives, you will live in this world.'

"'But I don't want to live without his love,' Parvati said.

"'He is a part of you, and you are love,' the siddha said. 'Remember what I have told you.' Then he rose with his dogs and walked out of the courtyard. That night Parvati made a special clasp for the jewel and wore it under her sari near her heart. The next day she was married to a man named Raja, who was my father. Raja never knew about Visnu or the visit from the siddha, at least not at first.

"Time passed and I was born and grew into a young woman. When I was sixteen, the same age my mother had been when she met Visnu, I met a man named Dharma and fell absolutely in love. For me Dharma was everything, the light in the sun and the moon, the wind through the trees. I loved him so much it was as if I was in love with God himself, that's how huge my devotion was. But unfortunately Dharma was also a Sudra, and there was no possibility of my marrying someone below my caste. But I was different from my mother. I told my parents that I was going to marry him and nothing would stop me. I swore I would die before I would let anyone stop me. Naturally, my father was shocked and outraged by my announcement. In ancient India a daughter simply didn't say things like that to her father. My mother tried to intervene, but he locked me in my room and wouldn't let me out. It is interesting that while all this was happening I had no knowledge of what my mother had gone through when she was my age. But I did have the yellow jewel the siddha had given my mother, on a gold chain near my heart. She had given it to me on my tenth birthday and told me always to keep it near, that it was magical.

"At this same time my grandmother, my mother's mother, came to my mother and told her about a dream she had when my mother had met Visnu. She told my mother, 'In the dream I learned you were supposed to be with that young man, that he was the one for you even though he was from another caste. But I was afraid to tell you in case you would marry him and bring disgrace to the entire family. I feel it is the same for poor Padma and her friend—they are meant for each other.'

"My mother was shocked because her mother had never even given her a sign that she knew about Visnu. But my grandmother knew a great deal. She told my mother she even knew the whereabouts of Visnu. My mother begged her to direct her to him, and the old woman did, although reluctantly, because she had the gift of prophecy and knew sorrow would come from their meeting again. She warned my mother of this, but she went to see Visnu anyway. How could she not?

"She found him a poor and unsuccessful man. He was living in the streets, in fact, and when she saw him he hadn't eaten in days. She had brought nuts and fruits and she fed him and they talked. He told her how happy he was to see her again and asked about her family. When she told him she had a daughter who was going through the same thing they had when they were young, he was sympathetic. Indeed, he felt as if she were talking about a daughter of his. He asked if it would be possible to see me and my mother said that the only way to accomplish this would be for him to go to our house as a simple laborer looking for work. Visnu agreed. Oh, this part is important: my mother told Visnu about the visit from the siddha and the magic gem he had given her. Visnu understood the deep significance of what the siddha had said. He had never stopped loving Parvati, even though his life had been very hard and lonely.

"Visnu headed for our house while my mother went to be with her mother for a day or two. But when Visnu got to our house my father told him that he didn't need any workers. At this Visnu confessed that he had known Parvati when he was young. In fact, he told my father the whole story—Visnu was such a pure soul that he was really incapable of lying. As you can imagine, my father was not pleased to have his wife's old love show up at his door, especially asking to see his daughter. My father ordered him to leave, and when Visnu was gone he came storming into my room. He asked me for my yellow gem and ripped it out of my hand. Then he locked my door. At the time I didn't know what was going on.

"My father was back not long afterward with ill tidings. My mother was dead. It seemed she had fallen into a sudden coma about the same time my father had taken the gem from me. My grandmother had brought us the news.

"That night my father had a dream, which I never fully heard, but it made him aware of the connection between the siddha's gem and the death of his wife. I know he questioned my grandmother about the gem, and she told him what she knew. What I do know for certain is that my father was suddenly anxious for me to take the gem back and wear it, in case I, too, died. But when I heard everything that had happened, and what my grandmother had to say, I understood the situation more clearly than my father. I refused to take the gem unless he agreed to my marrying Dharma.

" 'Don't you see?' I told my father. 'It wasn't the gem that kept my mother alive but the bond of love she had with Visnu. When in your anger you took the gem from me and ordered him away, you tried to break that bond. That is why she died. And I, too, even if I wear this gem constantly, will be as if dead if you don't let me marry Dharma. The gem's only magic is the love we bring to it.'

"My father then confessed to me a fear. He said, 'If you marry him you will leave and I will have no one to take care of me in my old age.' In those days children had to take care of their elderly parents. There was no one else to do it. I told him, 'Even if I marry Dharma I promise to stay with you until the day you die.' That made my father happy.

"But we still had the problem of our castes. The entire village would be angry if they heard about our union. But we had an advantage—Dharma was from a far-off region. No one in my town knew him or his family, and my father advised us to say that Dharma was a Brahmin. That of course was easier said than done because a Brahmin is taught many things from birth that a Sudra never learns: how to perform the *hotri* sacrifices and chant the *Gayatri* mantra and so on. But my father said he would teach Dharma all these things. For his part, Dharma was reluctant to lie. Like Visnu before him, he had an innocent nature. But I told him that it was better to lie and be together than never to see each other again. Finally Dharma said that he would be a Brahmin.

"So we were married and at first things went well. My joy at being with Dharma erased any fear I might have had of future discovery, or at least overshadowed it. My father began to teach Dharma everything he knew as a Brahmin, and Dharma was quick to learn. Everything seemed to be going according to plan. But then my father was suddenly taken ill and died. At the same time I learned I was pregnant. The timing was unfortunate because both Dharma and I knew that the father of a child was required to perform several public *pujas*, or ceremonies, at the birth of a child, particularly if it was a male child. Dharma was not ready to do the pujas. There was no one we trusted enough to ask to teach him. In private, he studied the holy Vedas and tried to learn what he needed, but much of the tradition of the Vedas is passed down orally. He could only get so much out of the books.

"The day came when our child was born, a boy

whom I named Bhrigu. He was an amazing child—
even as an infant he exuded great peace and light.
The entire village gathered to witness the pujas
done in honor of Bhrigu's coming into the world.
Dharma set everything up and bravely started. But
it was not long before a muttering went through the
crowd. Dharma was doing the pujas wrong, the
elders cried. His pronunciation of the chants, even
his movements in the rituals were wrong. They
called out that he could not possibly be a Brahmin,
and that our union must therefore be sinful.

"We were in a real bind. I was sitting in the
middle of all this with tiny Bhrigu on my lap and
Dharma staring at me as if he knew he should never
have agreed to this lie. The villagers were not going
to stone us to death—they were not that barbaric.
But they would drive us from the village without
any food or other supplies, and the end result
would probably have been the same as a stoning.
Certainly it would have been hard for Bhrigu and
me to survive in the wild. At the time there were a
lot of tigers in the surrounding forests. All looked
lost.

"But just then an amazing man came walking
into the village. I had never met him before but
intuitively I recognized him as the siddha my
mother had met the night before she was to be
married. He had about him an aura of complete
authority and grace. He strode right into the center
of the puja and stood behind me, placing one hand
on my head and the other on the child. Then he
spoke to the people.

" 'It is true that Dharma is not a Brahmin by

birth, and that this marriage, and therefore this child, are not sanctioned by the hymns of the Vedas. But the Vedas are much more than hymns, much greater than any words. They are the expressions of the divine, of love, and when Padma and Dharma met their love was so strong that they were willing to risk everything, including their lives, to be together. Such was the power of their love. Such was the power of the divine grace in their lives. And only because of that grace was it possible for this child to be born to them, this child you want to drive away.'

"The siddha stopped and picked up Bhrigu and held him up for all to see. 'This boy will grow up to be a great seer. It will be his special mission to bring people back to a true understanding of the Vedas. He will teach divine love and he will awaken the knowledge of God in the hearts of men and women everywhere. He will teach all people, regardless of caste. In fact, he will reshape much of what you understand as caste.' The siddha smiled at tiny Bhrigu. 'This small child, you will one day call him Master.'

"Then the siddha gave me back Bhrigu, and stared into Dharma's and my eyes, and then walked away and was gone. To say the villagers were shaken would be an understatement. The siddha had spoken with such great authority and he was so obviously an enlightened man that they didn't bother us any longer. We were left alone, although people were not friendly. But I didn't care. I had my husband and my son, and I was content, more so with each passing year. Because everything the siddha had foretold turned out to be true. My boy grew into a great saint, and I became his first disciple, and he taught me and the world many things, not the least of which was that all people are equal. It was this Master, my son, who led a great spiritual revival that swept over India in those ancient times. Even to this day Bhrigu's name can be found in the Vedas."

Ilonka stopped talking and sat back.

Everyone was staring at her. Spence spoke first.

"How do you know all that stuff about the Vedas?" he asked.

"I remember it," Ilonka said simply.

"Have you ever studied ancient Indian culture?" Kevin asked.

Ilonka shrugged. "I've read a few books on it, but there are things in my story that are not in the books."

"Then how do you know they're accurate?" Spence asked.

"I assume they are," Ilonka said.

"Did you read these books before you remembered this life, or after?" Spence asked.

Ilonka chuckled. "I know what you're really asking. Do I remember things from a past life that I am able to verify independently? The answer is— I'm not sure. I read books about India when I was little. More recently I read about it after having these past-life experiences. What I learned from the books and what I remember are blurred together in my mind, but I do know I have an understanding of

123

ancient India that the authors of the books do not."
She paused. "Does that make sense?"

"I would like to pin you down on a few specifics,"
Spence said. "For example, this son of yours—
Bhrigu. You say his name is in the Vedas?"

"That's right. I can show it to you."

"Did you see the name before you had this past
life come back to you?" Spence asked.

"I don't think so. It just came to me—his name,
everything about him."

"You don't think so, but you're not sure?"
Spence asked.

Ilonka yawned. She was glad she was through
with her story, she was feeling exhausted. "I
couldn't swear to it. Maybe I did see the name in
some book and forgot it. I told you, I'm not positive
these are past lives. I just feel they are. They may
simply be products of my imagination."

"Why all the analysis?" Sandra asked, her words
still a little slurred. "Let's just enjoy it and go on to
the next story."

"I liked your story very much, Ilonka," Anya
said softly, her head hanging heavy on her chest. "It
touched me."

"It was beautiful," Kevin agreed. "You're sure
you were Padma, and not another person in the
story?"

Ilonka smiled. He had asked a similar question
the night before. "Who else could I have been if I
weren't the heroine?" she asked.

Kevin smiled at the question. He took a drink of

water—he had drunk little of his wine—and cleared his throat. Ilonka was anxious for him to continue "The Magic Mirror," the tale of Herme and Teresa.

"When Herme left the Louvre with Teresa he realized he had no place to stay except with her. Even though Teresa was in love with him, she hadn't realized that when she invited him to come with her she was picking up a roommate. Teresa had no home either—she was staying at a youth hostel. You can sleep in them at night real cheap, but you have to be gone by nine in the morning, and you can't come back until sunset. They're often crowded and uncomfortable, and the one Teresa was staying in was particularly small. On top of all that Herme, of course, didn't have a cent or *centime.* He didn't own any clothes except the ones he had on. Teresa was puzzled by his lack of things, but she was so in love with him that she chose to help him as best she could. She was just happy to be with him because Herme's joy was a thing of great wonder. Teresa knew it wouldn't be long before Herme made a name for himself as a famous artist. But she wasn't with him because she knew he would be a success. But it had crossed her mind a number of times, which was natural—she was, after all, a poor young woman in need of some stability in life.

"At the youth hostel Teresa had to pay for both of them. In the morning she had to buy them breakfast. Herme really wanted breakfast because even though he had eaten with her in the Louvre he had done so to be polite, not because he was hungry. Now he was starving. He ate with great relish because everything tasted good to him.

"Teresa decided their first priority was to get Herme a job. She took Herme to a portrait studio where people came to have paintings of themselves and their families commissioned. But Herme had no samples of his work to show the man who owned the place. He couldn't very well point to a da Vinci as one of his works. The man told Herme to come back when he had something to show him, which was fine with Herme. Teresa was disappointed, though. She was going through her meager amount of money very quickly.

"But Paris is a wonderful city for artists, and walking along the streets Herme noticed many painters doing portraits right on the sidewalks. He told Teresa he would like to do that to make a living. Herme enjoyed being outside: the fresh air, the fall of the rain, the birds singing in the trees— everything was a delight to him. The only problem was that to buy supplies for Herme would exhaust the remainder of Teresa's money. But her faith in him was such that she got him what he needed: an easel, a chair, a few brushes, oils, and canvases. Herme set up his easel on a busy corner not far from the Louvre. Although he was happy to be outside the museum, he liked to see it. It reassured him in some way he didn't fully understand.

"Herme quickly attracted clients, his skill was so

great, his personality so delightful. The word went around about him and he had plenty of work, but it wasn't as if he made huge sums of money. If Paris is a haven for artists, it is also one of the most competitive places on earth for them to work. Herme could do wonderful portraits, but he was forced to hurry them. It was not the way he was used to working. In the past he had always molded paintings slowly. As a result of his working quickly the quality of his work suffered, although it was still far above most of what was being done. After a couple of months working on the streets, Teresa had saved enough of his money to open up a studio for him. It was Teresa who took care of all the business details—Herme had no head for money. But he was happy with his life. He was still so much in love with Teresa. Kissing her, touching her, making love to her—these things were so new and exciting to him that he didn't for a moment regret his decision to become mortal.

"With a studio he was able to settle into a routine, which didn't help his work. He missed being outside, and he soon tired of doing simple portraits. He was an ex-angel who helped to inspire the greatest paintings known to mankind. He wanted to branch out and paint other things, but Teresa told him that was not possible. He had clients booked months in advance, and she had already taken deposits from them and he had to paint them—end of discussion. Herme went along with her advice because he understood she knew much more about the world than he did. Also, he disliked disagreeing with her because she could be stubborn and she would argue until she got her way.

"During this time the two of them began to make substantial money, even though they were still far from rich. Teresa found them a nice apartment in a rich section of town and furnished it with antiques. Herme continued to work each day, often on the weekends as well, and did one portrait after another. Then for the first time he began to receive complaints about his work. People were no longer impressed by everything he did—the reasons varied. He had begun to charge more money, or Teresa had, and naturally the demands of his clientele had gone up. These people were paying more and they expected to get more in return. Also, as I already mentioned, he was taking on too many clients and was having to rush. Finally, though, and probably the main reason was that he was beginning to feel stale and uninspired. It was the unseen qualities that Herme had always brought out in his subjects that made his portraits so special. Now he was painting only what he saw on the surface.

"Teresa would hear the complaints and in turn complained to Herme that he had to do better. But when he told her he needed a change of scenery she was open to the idea. Teresa had not given up on her dream of going to America, and she suggested to Herme that they move to New York. He was delighted, even though it would mean he'd be leaving the Louvre, possibly forever. He continued to go back to the museum when he wasn't feeling his best, and would wander its long halls, gazing upon past glories. He still loved Teresa as much as ever, and he could see she still loved him, but he wasn't as happy as he had been the day he left the museum. He wondered if it was because their love had lost much of its spontaneity, its enthusiasm. He wasn't sure because he could no longer see into Teresa's heart—into anybody's heart—as well as he had been able to in the past.

"They sold their studio and apartment and moved to New York City, and for a time things were better between them. Herme was not working at first and they were able to spend more time together. Their romance underwent a brief revival, but then suddenly it swung the other way. Teresa was not used to having Herme around constantly, and he had taken up the bad habit of clinging to her, something Teresa couldn't stand. Of course Herme only began to cling to her when he felt her withdrawing. He had no previous experience in human relationships. He thought the best way to combat her waning love was to pour more love her way. But this made him act strained around her, and Herme's greatest charm had always been his natural spontaneity, his ease in every situation. Now that charm was failing him and he didn't know how to act.

"Teresa wanted Herme to start working again, but he was reluctant to do portraits. He wanted to get outside to capture the many natural tapestries the earth had to offer. He also wanted to try more abstract works. What this did was put him in competition with thousands of other struggling artists in America. He was giving up his area of expertise in favor of his ideals. It goes without saying that his decision didn't thrill Teresa. She argued that they were going through their savings and that she was not going back to living hand to mouth. In fact, she said that he owed her, that she had given him his start when he had had nothing. Herme was incapable of responding to her accusations, except by withdrawing more and more. He took to going for long walks through New York City late at night. Many times he wouldn't return home until the sun was up.

"But one night he came back early and found Teresa was not alone. Despite everything that had happened to him since he had left the Louvre, he was still incredibly naïve. He had never imagined that *his* Teresa could want another man. He came home to find the only woman he had ever loved in bed with another man."

"How horrible," Anya whispered, and it was almost as if she did so involuntarily. Ilonka glanced at her but Anya did not return her look, lowering her head as if she were deep in thought.

Kevin nodded. "It was a nightmare for Herme. He saw the man, yet he only focused on Teresa. But what could she say to him? She just swore and turned her head away. Herme didn't know what to do. He walked out of his apartment. Always, even since becoming mortal, he had felt a light inside that guided his movements. But now that light had gone out and he found the darkness unbearable. He wandered into sections of New York he had never been to before, parts where it was as easy to buy a knife in the back as it was a handful of drugs. He hoped someone would attack him, shoot him, stab him, put him out of his misery. But no one came near him because he was in such despair. It was as if he weren't human anymore, merely a wraith sent from the netherworld to haunt humanity. He felt that way, a stain on the planet. He walked until he reached Brooklyn Bridge and moved out to the center of it, above the icy winter water. He climbed over the rail and he stared down. He saw nothing beneath him except blackness and felt nothing above him. But he didn't call out to God or pray for release. He was past the point of caring, so he thought. He planned to kill himself and be done with it.

"Yet just before he jumped he remembered back to the day he had first left the Louvre: his joy, his excitement, and most of all, his love. And he wondered where it had all gone, and if Teresa had as much to do with what he had lost as he believed. For he understood in that moment that it was his love that had made Teresa wonderful in his eyes. He understood that something inside him—and not just the outside circumstances—had changed. But what had that change been? It seemed obvious.

He had been an angel and had become mortal. He had been divine and had become human. But he wondered, as he stood on the rail of the bridge above the freezing water if it was not possible for a human to become divine, if it was not a two-way process. It was a funny thought, one he had never had before. But it touched him in some deep part of his soul. Yes, he felt he had a soul again. He climbed off the rail and back onto the main part of the bridge. He looked at the sky, seeing the stars shine through the smog above the city, and he felt blessed.

"Herme left the bridge. He went to rediscover what he had lost. He set out to find himself."

Kevin's voice had begun to fail him and he momentarily rested his head on his arms on top of the table. Ilonka watched anxiously until he sat back up and smiled at everyone. He reached for his glass and took a sip of water.

"That's all for tonight," he said.

"Couldn't you finish it?" Anya asked, with surprising feeling. "Please?"

He shook his head and coughed. "I don't think I could if I wanted to. I'm tired."

Ilonka yawned again, so loudly she embarrassed herself. "I'm exhausted, too. I feel like I could go to sleep in this seat." She tapped Kevin's arm in approval. "I am happy you're last. Who could compete? That was fabulous."

"Does it end happily?" Anya asked, not giving up.

"If I tell you the end you'll have nothing to look forward to," Kevin said.

Anya stared at him oddly, almost as if to say *I have nothing to look forward to.*

"Herme sounds like the kind of guy who could have benefited greatly from my counsel," Spence said.

"I love Herme," Sandra said, playing with her wineglass. "He reminds me of Dan. They both loved nature."

"Oh, brother," Spence said.

Ilonka had not been exaggerating her exhaustion. A heavy hand of fatigue lay across her head, its fingers probing deep into the centers of her brain. The weariness surprised her; she had, after all, taken a nap that afternoon. She decided that the trip to the hospital, and her confrontation with Kathy, had taken more out of her than she realized. She continued to worry that Kevin must know what she had told Kathy. Yet when he looked at her during the evening there was only fondness in his eyes. He continued to stare at her now.

"Are you walking me home tonight?" he asked.

She smiled. "It's your turn, buster." The words were no sooner out of her mouth than she regretted them. He didn't have the strength to walk her up to the second floor. She hastily touched his arm again. "That's all right. I want to walk you back to your room."

"Don't be out too late," Spence warned them.

Ilonka stood up. "Yes, Dad."

"I'd like to have a few words with you before you leave," Spence said to Anya.

"Wheel me to my room," Anya said. "Good

133

night, Sandra. I'm glad you got laid at least once in your life. Good night, Kevin. I hope your Herme gets his wings back before the mud of the world drags him any lower." Anya suddenly glanced around the study. "It's been great meeting here," she said with feeling.

"We'll have a great meeting tomorrow night," Spence told her.

Anya blinked, her gaze far off. "Yeah. Tomorrow."

Kevin was having difficulty walking, an unexpected side effect of his leukemia. He said he had awakened that morning with a numbness in his left leg. He had to lean on her the whole way back. He invited her inside for tea, which meant a lot to her. Only she was too tired to accept the invitation.

"Maybe tomorrow night," she said, putting her hand over her mouth to stifle another yawn. She leaned on the wall for support, as Kevin did. What a fine pair they made, she thought. "After we've found out what became of Herme."

"You know, I thought about you when I was working on the story," he said.

She laughed. "I hope you didn't pattern Teresa after me."

"Would that offend you?"

"Yeah. She cheated on her guardian angel. I would never do that."

"Do you believe in angels, Ilonka?"

She loved his saying her name. He could spend the night whispering it in her ear and she would have been content. She thought of Anya's last comment to Sandra, about her having had sex at least once. Ilonka had never slept with a boy in her life. She had never wanted to until she met Kevin. It was lovely to be talking with him just before going to bed, but suddenly she was filled with a profound sadness that she might die never having been touched, caressed. She had no idea what it would actually be like to make love. And that's all she had wanted out of her life: to matter to someone more than anything else.

Where was her Master now? What would he say to her grief? How come he wasn't with her now, in this, her hardest of all lives?

"I believe in angels," she whispered. *I believe in you.*

"Ilonka?"

She closed her eyes and put her hand to her head. "I have to go to bed."

He hugged her gently. "Go to bed."

He would say your love is nothing if it is based on a lie.

"I saw Kathy today," she said in his ear.

He let go of her and stared at her. The hallway was dark; she couldn't read his expression. But she could hear the understanding in his voice.

"I know," he said.

"I—"

"It doesn't matter." He pressed a finger to her lips. "Don't think about it."

Her eyes were damp. "I was cruel."

135

"This situation is cruel." He leaned over and kissed her on the forehead. "Sleep. Dream about your Master. He fascinates me."

She was pleased. "Really?"

Kevin opened his door and limped inside. "Really, Ilonka. But wouldn't he say to us—what is reality? Good night."

"Good night, my love," she whispered after he had closed his door. She had never told Kevin that her Master constantly challenged her to discriminate between what was real and what was illusion.

She found Spence in her room sitting on her bed across from Anya, who was still in her wheelchair. Ilonka had the feeling she was walking in at a bad time and would have excused herself except she honestly felt she was going to collapse. She plopped down on her bed at Spence's back.

"Ignore me, I'm just a blob of protoplasm," she mumbled, her eyes closed. She felt Spence stand up.

"I should be going," he said uneasily.

"You can go," Anya said, her tone curiously authoritative.

Ilonka heard the door open and close.

"Ilonka?" Anya said.

"Yes?" she whispered.

"I never told anyone about Bill before."

"Yes."

"I told you because I trust you."

"Yes."

There was a long pause. Ilonka might have dozed

136

in the middle of it, she wasn't sure. When Anya spoke next she sounded a thousand miles away.

"I know Kevin's in each of your past-life stories. I think he knows it, too. But the past is the past, you know. It's dead. I hope you two get to live a little before we're all dead." Anya paused and Ilonka heard a faint movement. She felt the touch of something warm and moist on her cheek and wondered if Anya had kissed her. "Dream, my darling," Anya said softly.

"This is all a dream," Ilonka whispered. Then she was gone.

She sat with the Master in a lush forest. The sun hung low at the tops of the trees, perhaps ready to set, maybe beginning to rise. Time seemed frozen in the eternal moment. The orange light in the Master's hair was beautiful, as were his dark eyes, those eyes that saw all things and never judged. He played with the beads around his neck as she came to the conclusion of her long, sad story.

"How do you feel right now?" he asked suddenly.

She shrugged, confused. "I just told you. My life is in ruins."

"Yes. Your life is in ruins. But how do you feel right now?"

"I feel wonderful sitting here with you. But—"

"There is no but," he interrupted. "There is just now. Your mind dwells in the past. You feel regret about what you have done, anger over what you feel has been done to you. Or else your mind is anxious

about the future. But the past is past and the future doesn't exist. All you have is right now and right now you feel fine." He smiled so sweetly, the flash of his love. "So what is your problem? You have no problem."

"But—"

"There is no but." He snapped his fingers near her head. "Be in the present moment. Be here with me totally. I am here with you totally. That is enlightenment, nothing more."

"But I cannot be with you always," she cried. "I have to go back to my life and my life is hard. I have no one to love me, no one to take care of me. I am alone in the world."

"You are not alone. I am with you always."

"I know that but I don't always feel that." She began to weep. "My pain is real for me. Words cannot erase it."

"Certainly words cannot heal. Only silence can do that. So what can I say to you to make you feel better? You want me to work a miracle on you?"

She nodded. "I need a miracle."

The Master considered. "All right, I will give you a miracle. When you return home everything will be perfect for you. Your life will be just as it should be."

She looked at him doubtfully, for she knew how he loved to joke with her. "Are you promising me that?" she asked.

"I give you my word. And if you believe in my word, if you have that faith, then you will see that everything is already perfect. God gives you what you need in life to learn. He continues to give you *hard lessons because you are a slow learner. I am not saying you can't make mistakes. Mistakes are all right. But you keep making the same ones."*

She shook her head sadly. *"I want him back."*

"He is gone. He is dead."

She took the Master's hand. *"But you can do anything. I have seen your power. Please bring him back to me?"*

The Master stared at her gravely. *"Be careful what you wish of me. You might get it."*

CHAPTER V

IN THE MORNING ILONKA OPENED HER EYES AND STARED at the ceiling for the longest time. During that time she hardly had a thought, except that her head felt strangely full. She wondered briefly if it was because of the little wine she had drunk the night before. Finally she rolled over to see how Anya was doing. Anya was always awake before her, and Ilonka usually found her reading in the morning.

Anya was still sound asleep, flat on her back.

Ilonka glanced at the clock. Wow—ten in the morning. If ever there were two sleepyheads, it was them. Ilonka continued to stare at Anya. She was really sleeping deeply, she was so still. It made Ilonka nervous how still she was.

"Anya?" Ilonka said. "Anya?"

No answer. Ilonka slowly sat up, her eyes never leaving her friend's face.

"Anya? It's ten in the morning. Wake up."

Still as a mannequin. Anya was hardly breathing.

"Anya?" Ilonka stepped over to her bed and shook the girl. "Anya."

No, not *hardly*. Not at all. Anya had stopped breathing.

"Anya!" Ilonka cried. Frantic, she felt Anya's neck for a pulse.

Nothing.

"Anya!" Ilonka shook her hard and the poor girl rocked back and forth like a bag of old clothes. Their bedroom window was cracked a few inches; the roar of the surf could be heard in the distance. The room was chilly; Anya's skin was as cold as the bare floor. Her friend had been dead for several hours. There was no chance of resuscitating her, not that the staff at the hospice would have tried anyway. They were in a place to die. The only way to officially check out was to check out for good.

Tears stung Ilonka's eyes. "Anya, no," she whispered, hugging her, holding her, kissing her. It was inevitable, she knew, they would all go this way sooner or later. Yet Ilonka was numb with shock. It was as if she knew nothing about death until this moment. She missed Anya already.

After some time she left her friend and staggered downstairs to Dr. White's office. The gentleman was just coming out of his room when he saw Ilonka. He immediately rushed to her side. She realized she had no robe on.

"Ilonka," he said. "What's wrong?"

"Anya died during the night."

Dr. White embraced her. "I am sorry. Is she still in her bed?"

"Yes."

"Let me go see her."

Ilonka let go of him. "I'll come with you."

"Are you sure?"

"Yes. I should—help take care of her."

Ilonka had left Anya with her arms folded across her chest. Dr. White reached for one wrist and checked for a pulse. Finding none, he opened one of her eyes and peered into it. Ilonka briefly turned her head away. Finally he pressed his palm on her forehead, no doubt attempting to make a rough guess at her body temperature.

Body.

That's what she was now. Not a person. Not a young woman with hopes and dreams, but a dead body. Toward the end Anya had abandoned all her dreams. She was more accepting of her fate than any of them, yet that acceptance was not something Ilonka wanted to emulate. Not yet, at least, not today.

"She is dead, isn't she?" Ilonka asked. It was a stupid question if ever there was one, but she needed to be absolutely sure.

"Yes," Dr. White said, feeling Anya's muscle tone on her arms and legs. "I would say she has been dead for seven or eight hours."

Seven or eight hours ago would have placed her death not long after they had gone to bed. So soon after the lights went off. It made Ilonka wonder.

"Couldn't you finish it? Please?"

When had Anya ever begged for anything in her life?

"It's been great meeting here."

Said like she was saying goodbye to the study.

"I never told anyone about Bill before."

Said like a confession.

Then there was the kiss.

"Dream, darling."

"What did she die of?" Ilonka asked.

Dr. White glanced at her as if to say, Yes, you are upset and you can ask one stupid question, but that is two in a row. "She died of cancer," he said.

"I mean specifically."

"I am being specific."

Ilonka shook her head. "Anya was talking freaky last night."

"What are you suggesting?"

"Nothing."

"Ilonka?"

"I'm suggesting that maybe she killed herself. She was always taking so many drugs. I think you should do an autopsy."

Dr. White sighed. "There will be no autopsy. I wouldn't recommend it, and the family wouldn't approve of it."

"She hardly has any family, and why wouldn't you recommend it?"

Dr. White moved away from Anya's body and touched her arm. "Let's step outside and talk about this."

"I want to talk about it here."

"All right, Ilonka. What does it matter how she died? She was in terrible pain in the end. Now she is out of pain. That's all that should matter to us who cared for her."

"It isn't all that matters." Ilonka was in tears again. "How she died is important to me. She was my friend. I don't want to—" She couldn't finish.

"You don't want to what?"

I don't want to end the same way she did.

"Nothing." She was being unreasonable and she knew it. Yet there was something important here that she was missing, something that went beyond the possibility that Anya might have ended her life intentionally with an overdose of drugs. It was there, at the tip of her fingers, she just couldn't get ahold of it.

"It is unlikely that she killed herself with an overdose," Dr. White said, watching her.

"How do you know?"

"An overdose generally takes a while to kill someone. If she did die between two and three in the morning, she would have had to have taken the drugs before your club met. I assume she was at the meeting?"

"Yes."

"Then suicide is unlikely here. Had she swallowed enough drugs to kill her by early morning, she would have been unconscious at the meeting."

What he said sounded logical. Yet Ilonka continued to be plagued by uncertainty. "Is there another possibility we're overlooking?" she asked.

"Such as?"

"I don't know, I'm asking you."

Dr. White looked unhappy. "Are you asking these questions because you don't want to deal with the real issue here, Ilonka? Your roommate has died—she has been close to death for some time now. It's a shock to you, especially considering your own grave illness."

"Have you gotten any word on my tests?" she asked suddenly.

"No."

Ilonka reached out and took Anya's hand, not because she wanted to but because she felt she should. "I loved Anya," she said. "But I never told her that."

"I'm sure she knew," Dr. White said gently.

Ilonka shook her head, remembering her story of Bill the previous afternoon. Now there would be no point in contacting him. "No. I'm sure Anya Zimmerman was one of those people who *didn't* know she was loved."

"I have to contact what family she has left. I will move the body from here as quickly as possible."

"Where will you put it?" She was just wondering.

"In the basement, for the present." He paused. "Would you like to gather her personal items together?"

Ilonka understood the source of the question. Space was a valuable commodity. The body and its belongings had to be moved out so that another living body could be moved in quickly. She thought it would feel weird for the next girl to be sleeping in a bed where someone had just died. It was hard enough for Ilonka to think she had slept most of the night next to a dead body. Of course, in this place, someone had died in each of their beds before they had arrived. It was a sobering thought.

"I can get her things together," Ilonka said.

Dr. White left to take care of business. Only a few minutes later a couple of nurses arrived for the body. Ilonka was still holding on to Anya's hand. Time to say goodbye—not easy to do. The nurses covered her with a green sheet and lifted her onto a gurney and wheeled her out. Ilonka was left alone with her pain. She didn't know if the others in the club knew what had happened. She should be the one to tell them, though. Soon. But not just this second, she thought.

Ilonka went into the bathroom to collect Anya's toothpaste and hairbrush and stuff like that. Only it wasn't there.

"What?" Ilonka whispered to herself.

All of Anya's toiletries were gone.

But that's not possible. She just died. Who would have taken them? Who could have taken them with me here?

The answer, to both questions, was no one.

Could it be the sign? Could Anya be telling her there was an afterlife?

No way, it's just a matter of timing. One of the nurses heard Anya was dead while I was talking to Dr. White and immediately cleaned out the cupboards. No, maybe not. Only I knew she was dead and I only talked to Dr. White for ten seconds before we returned to the room. OK, it's a trick. Anya knew she was going to kill herself so she gathered everything up in the middle of the night and stowed it elsewhere to fool me. That's it! She heard my story

146

about Delius and Mage and Shradha. What better sign to fake me out with?

The only problem with the second hypothesis was that Anya had been a grievously ill girl who also happened to be crippled. It would have been next to impossible for her to gather all her things together and dispose of them in the middle of the night. Anya couldn't even wheel her chair from one place to another without assistance.

Then what? Ilonka didn't know.

It was time to talk to the others.

CHAPTER VI

WORD TRAVELED FAST IN THE HOSPICE. THE OTHERS already knew Anya was dead by the time Ilonka reached them. The four remaining members of the club—Ilonka, Sandra, Spence, and Kevin—had gathered in the boys' room. There they tried to console themselves by repeatedly saying that it was probably for the best, that Anya had been in more pain than any mortal should have to withstand. Spence was the hardest hit by the loss. Ilonka had never seen him weep before. Then again, he had been the closest to Anya in many ways. Certainly he had fought the most with her.

Everyone in the group denied having touched Anya's personal items. The nurses, also, said they knew nothing about them. The four of them just stared at one another and shook their heads. Ilonka didn't believe any of them were lying. No one knew what to think. It was decided, though, that they would investigate the matter more fully.

Then, before they could begin to discuss if a sign from beyond the grave had been sent by Anya, another rumor swept the hospice, going to every quarter of the huge mansion. It originated from the nurses' station, but before it could be verified, head nurse Schratter put a clamp on it. She said there would be no comment until Dr. White returned. Apparently he had left the hospice in an attempt to find somebody from Anya's family. The rumor was a powerful one.

One of the patients at the hospice had been misdiagnosed.

That person was not going to die.

When Ilonka heard the rumor, she knew it had to be her.

She was being logical, she thought she was. Because she was the only one in the hospice who had recently gone for tests. She was the only one who had new data coming in on her. She laughed out loud at the news because they had all wanted to laugh at her when she'd insisted on another scan. It was as if a great weight were suddenly lifted; she couldn't believe her joy, even in the midst of Anya's tragedy. She also knew it had to be her because as soon as the words reached her ears, her pain level dropped considerably. Why, the eternal cramp in her abdomen even lessened and she was able to take a deep breath for the first time in a couple of months. She realized a lot of her discomfort had been in her head. She could hardly wait for Dr. White to return to the hospice.

I am not going to die! I am going to live! Live! Live! Live!

Ilonka heard the news when she was alone in her

room. Another patient—she didn't even know his name—told her as he swept up and down the hall on the second floor. Immediately, though, in conjunction with her relief, she felt bad for the others in the group, especially Kevin, her dear Kevin. How could she just leave him in this place to die? She couldn't; she made a vow to herself to remain until he died. Dr. White would understand; he wouldn't turn her out.

Another search of her room had failed to turn up any of Anya's personal items.

Ilonka kept looking over her shoulder as she searched.

She closed the window. There seemed to be a cold draft in the room.

Finally about three in the afternoon, she decided to return to Kevin's room. She found him alone, sitting on his bed flipping through sketches in a huge notepad. He was probably doing more than browsing; he had a pencil in his right hand. But he closed the pad as soon as she entered and she didn't get a chance to see what he was working on. Apparently Spence was out mailing a long letter to his lady love, Caroline. Kevin said he was forever writing her; it took up half his days.

"It's nice that he has someone," Ilonka said. She sat across from Kevin on Spence's bed.

"Yeah," Kevin said thoughtfully.

Ilonka hesitated. "I wanted to talk to you more about what happened with Kathy."

"I should have told her a long time ago. You spared me the trauma."

"You would have broken it to her gently. I came at her like a raving bitch."

"Sometimes you have to be cruel to be kind."

"I assume you've talked to her, then?" she asked.

"Yes."

"Will she be visiting again soon?"

"I don't think so," he said.

"I had no right."

Kevin raised his hand. "It's fine, really. Let's not talk about it anymore." He shook his head. "I can't believe Anya won't be there tonight. It won't be the same."

"Should we even meet?"

"I think Anya would want us to. Maybe she'll give us another sign."

"Do you think she's given us a sign already?"

Kevin eyed her curiously. "Since the sign is related to a story you told, what do *you* think?"

"I'm intrigued."

"Nothing more?"

"So much is happening all of a sudden, I haven't had a chance to really sit and think about it." She paused. "You heard the rumor that's going around?"

"That one of us isn't terminal? Yeah, it sounds like more than a rumor. I understand everyone's just waiting to find out who it is."

"Kevin."

"What?"

"It's me."

His face brightened. "Really? Dr. White told you? I didn't know he was back yet."

151

"He isn't back, but I know it's me. Who else could it be?"

Kevin's face darkened. "Ilonka, don't you think you're jumping to a dangerous conclusion?"

She laughed. "I'm not jumping that far. Look, I went for a scan yesterday. They said they would have the results back today. Suddenly, today, one person at this hospice is no longer terminal."

Kevin nodded. "I admit it is a possibility. I'll keep my fingers crossed for you." He turned and glanced out the window. The curtains were pulled back although the window was closed. As usual, the temperature in the room was elevated. "I would love to see the ocean again," he said.

She gestured to his left leg. "Is it still numb?"

"Not as bad as yesterday. Sometime in the middle of the night it seemed to wake up again, at least partially." He considered. "Would you like to go for a walk with a cripple?"

Ilonka smiled. "I would love to go anywhere with you. You can lean on me for support." She stood up. "Let me get my coat. I'll be back in a minute. You bundle up warm."

Ten minutes later found them walking along the edge of the wide lawn that led down to the rocky cliff. The weather was dismal: gray clouds, cutting gusts. The waves were a fury, the salty spray reaching them even though they stayed in the grassy area. Walking with Kevin was not the easiest thing. His left leg may have been better, but he was leaning on her for half his support. He finally pointed to a boulder and the two of them settled down. Ilonka tied Kevin's scarf tighter. He was shivering.

"We shouldn't stay out here long," she said.

He gestured to the churning surf. "It's amazing, isn't it? The power of nature. You know, I sometimes feel sorry for myself that my life should be cut short, then I look out over the sea and think, this world is over four billion years old. The life of a man or woman who lives to a hundred is just a flash of lightning compared to that time scale. Then I don't feel so bad. I feel honored that I got to come here at all." He drew in a deep breath and surveyed the coast. "It's a beautiful world."

"Is there anything special that you miss?" she asked.

He nodded. "I miss having the energy to paint, to run, to go to school. I really enjoyed getting up and going to class every morning. I know that sounds weird, but I enjoyed learning."

"It doesn't sound weird to me. Anything else?"

He smiled, blushing. "I miss the things Herme missed being an angel."

"Are you Herme? You said I was Teresa."

"I never said that."

"You compared me to that cheating bitch. But I forgive you." She paused. "So you miss the love of a woman?"

He didn't answer her directly. "One of the reasons I'm telling that story is for you."

She was startled. "Really? Am I supposed to learn something from it?"

"I didn't say that either." He shrugged. "The story just reminds me of us."

She blinked. She wasn't sure she had heard him correctly. "Of you and me?"

He looked at her. "Yes."

He likes me. I love him. Maybe he loves me.

Ilonka reached out and ran her hand through his thinning hair. In that moment, staring into his eyes, she was totally happy, more happy than she had ever been in her entire life.

"I would have let you paint whatever you wanted," she said.

"I would have enjoyed painting you."

She smiled. "Is that who you were sketching when I walked in on you a few minutes ago?"

"No. I was sketching the face of your Master."

She drew in a sharp breath. "But how?"

"I think I know what he looks like. Different in different lives, and yet always the same, too." He squeezed her hand. "When you tell your stories, I remember them with you. I remember Delius and Padma as if they were sitting beside me in the study next to the fire."

She chuckled with delight. "You should remember Shradha and Dharma better. You were supposed to—" She caught herself quickly. "I mean, you remind me of them more than the other two."

Kevin continued to stare at her, a look of surprise on his face. "I don't know," he said, chuckling.

"What don't you know?"

"I didn't know that." His eyes left hers for the ocean again. He shook from the cold and coughed.

"I want to ask you a favor. It's not a pleasant thing, but I would appreciate it if you could do it for me."

"Anything."

"I have told my parents that I want to be cremated and they have agreed. But they still want to bury my ashes somewhere and I don't want that. I don't want my mother to have a place to go to mourn. It won't be good for her. I don't even want her to know where my ashes are. But I have asked them to give them to you."

The topic distressed her. "To me?"

"Yes. I want you to take them here." He gestured to the cliff, to the waves. "I want you to throw them into the breeze above the water. I just want to blow away and be gone."

There were tears in her eyes. "But you won't just be gone. Maybe you won't die."

He regarded her closely. "I am going to die. I will be dead soon. Nothing can stop that. It is better to accept the reality. Didn't the Master say that once?"

She sniffed. "I believe he said it many times." She nodded. "I'll do it for you, Kevin. Can I sing as I do it? I like to sing."

"Sing to me now while I can still hear you."

"But the wind—you'll hardly be able to hear me."

"That's OK. You probably have a lousy voice."

She socked him lightly. "You may be able to paint like an angel, but I can sing like one."

"Go ahead."

"No." She took his arm. "Later. You have to get inside now. You're shaking like a leaf."

Ilonka led Kevin back to his room. She felt on top of the world, even though her boyfriend stood at death's door. But at least she could think of him as her boyfriend. *"The story just reminds me of us."* Us—there wasn't a bigger word that could have come out of his mouth.

At the same time she knew she was being ridiculous.

He's your boyfriend? He hasn't even kissed you on the lips. And he is going to be dead in a matter of days. There won't be a chance for him to kiss you. There won't be a chance for anything except for you to sing to his ashes.

She wished she had sung a few words for him.

Walking back to her room, she passed Sandra's room. She poked her head inside, a hello on her lips. But the word died on a suddenly icy breath. Sandra had her suitcase open on top of her bed. She was walking around her room, a smile on her face, singing as she packed.

No one at Rotterham Hospice ever repacked.

The nurses always did it for you.

After you were dead.

Ilonka took her head out of the room and slowly backed away from Sandra. The cold in her breath traveled down into her chest, into her heart, until she was pumping blood that was turning to ice shards that cut as they squeezed through her constricted veins. Yes, she suddenly felt as if she were bleeding inside in the worst way. She backed right into Spence.

"Hello, Ilonka," he said.

She turned to face him. "Is Dr. White back?"

"Yes. He's in his office. Do you know—"

She didn't wait to hear the rest of his question. She ran down the hall toward the doctor's office, forgetting that she was sick and that she hadn't run in over a year. She arrived at Dr. White's door gasping for breath. She didn't even bother to knock, she just barged in. He was sitting at his desk, studying some papers. He glanced up.

"Is it me?" she asked. "Is it Sandra? Who is it?"

"Ilonka." He stood up and gestured to one of the two chairs in front of his desk. "Have a seat. Relax."

She strode into the room, her fists clenched. "I don't want to relax. I want to live. Tell me, is Sandra the one who was misdiagnosed or was it me?"

He looked her straight in the eye. "It was Sandra. There are a couple types of Hodgkin's disease. Her doctor made an error. Her type is not fatal. She will be leaving the hospice today."

Ilonka just nodded, still breathing hard. "All right. That's good. That's fine. I'm happy for her. Did you get the results back on my tests?"

Dr. White gestured again. "Please sit down, Ilonka."

"I don't want to sit down! Just tell me the truth and be done with it!"

Dr. White picked up the paper on his desk. "I received the results by fax a few minutes ago. I was about to call you in. They are not encouraging. Your tumors have spread. Your spleen and liver are now seriously affected by the disease. There are also spots on your lungs." He put down the paper. "I'm sorry."

She just kept nodding. "All right, what does that mean? Does it mean I'm going to die? I guess that's what you're saying. All right, how long do I have to live?"

"Ilonka."

"How long, dammit?"

Dr. White sighed. "A couple of weeks, maybe."

She couldn't stop panting. "Maybe. Maybe two weeks. Maybe two days. How about maybe two years? I could do a lot in two years, you know. I could get a life. I could go to school and learn to sing properly. I could get a job and help disadvantaged people. I could get a boyfriend. I've never had a boyfriend, you know. I'm still a virgin. Imagine that in this day and age, huh? I'm going to die a virgin." Her voice cracked. "I'm going to die."

"Ilonka." Dr. White hurried from around his desk to comfort her. But she would have none of it. She shoved him away.

"I'm not Ilonka! I'm just a corpse waiting to lie still! Leave me alone!"

She ran from his office. She ran without knowing where she was going. Past the nurses' station. Past the oil paintings. She ran down what seemed an endless black tunnel. It should have been no surprise that she ended up in the darkest of all places.

The basement of Rotterham Hospice.

Where they kept the bodies before they disposed of them.

She came to her senses standing beside Anya.

They had put her dear friend in a green plastic bag.

There was a nametag on the outside.

Tagged and ready to deliver into oblivion.

Suddenly there was nothing more important to Ilonka in the whole universe than how Anya's personal items had vanished. She embraced the bag, hugging it to her chest.

"Are you still there?" she asked, weeping. "Is anything there?"

Why, God? Why do you give us life just so that you can take it from us?

"There's nothing," she whispered to the green plastic bag.

Ilonka did not know how long she stood there holding on to Anya's body. But a time came when she became aware of a hand on her shoulder. She turned and saw it belonged to Kevin. His brown eyes looked at her with such compassion that she felt as if he were touching her heart with hands made of an angel's light. But he did not say anything to her. He took her by the hand and led her upstairs to her room, limping the whole way, quite badly, but not leaning on her for support. He helped her into her bed, and then Dr. White came into the room and gave her a shot in the arm. The needle went in cold but the fluid that squirted from it was warm. The warmth spread through her body, a profound drowsiness filled her. Kevin stayed with her as she fell asleep. The last thing she saw was his face. The first thing she dreamed of was the Master's face.

"Master," she said. "What is it like to die?"

"Why do you ask?" the Master said. "Every night you go to sleep. You sleep and you don't know who you are. But every morning you wake up."

"But when I go to sleep I know I will wake up in the morning. When I die I don't know if I will be reborn. Will I?"

"The real you is never reborn, nor does it ever die. But the personality and the body is another matter. You believe you are this personality, this body. You think of yourself as clever with words and attractive with your long dark hair. But these things are not you. They are always changing. The real you never changes. The enlightened seldom speak of birth and rebirth. They are concerned with the present moment. If you are fully alive now, it is enough. You don't have to think about death. Death will come when it is supposed to come. We don't have to go chasing after it. You will cast off one set of clothes and put on another. It is no cause for concern."

"But I still don't want to die. I'm afraid of death."

"Do you want to have the same personality you have now for the rest of eternity?"

She had to laugh. "I would like to improve it first before it was made eternal."

The Master laughed with her. "You make it perfect and you will see that it ceases to exist. You think I am so powerful and wise. I tell you I am no one. That is how I understand everyone. I am like the sun, I shine the same on everyone. You are the sun. You are not this personality and body. Remember that when the time of death approaches and you will have no fear. This is a great secret I give you." He paused and spoke seriously. "Remember, too, that I will be with you at that time."

Chapter VII

SHE AWOKE IN THE DARK. EVEN BEFORE SHE OPENED HER eyes, or heard a sound, she knew he was still there. "How long have I been out?" she asked.

"It's close to midnight," Kevin said.

She opened her eyes and rolled over. He was sitting propped up with pillows on Anya's bed. He had on his red flannel robe; he had been dressed differently when she had been given the shot. He must have gone back to his room and changed. A shaft of moonlight came through the filmy curtains and shone on the floor, so she could see his face, although not clearly.

"It's time for another meeting," she said.

"I don't think there's going to be one tonight. Anya's gone and Sandra—she's gone, too. She came to say goodbye but you were asleep. She told me to tell you she'd write."

"She didn't waste any time in getting out of here, did she? I suppose I can't blame her." She sat up. "Thank you for staying with me. If you want to go to your room, I understand."

He shrugged. "I'd like to sit and talk if you don't mind."

"What would you like to talk about? How I made a fool of myself this afternoon? I should have listened to your warning."

"You are too hard on yourself, Ilonka. You're allowed to make mistakes. Everybody does."

"Except I keep making the same mistakes. That's not good. That's what the Master I told you about would say."

"Did you dream about him just now?" Kevin asked.

"Yes. How did you know that?"

"Because I dozed when you were asleep and I think I dreamed about him, too. But I don't remember much from the dream except that it was wonderful to sit with him."

"I remember my dream. He spoke to me about death, how it was nothing to fear."

"Are you afraid to die?" Kevin asked.

"Yes. Especially now that I know it is so near. Aren't you?"

He smiled. "Not since you told your stories."

"Seriously."

"I am serious. I told you I felt like I was in those places and times with you. And I feel that even when I leave this body I will be somewhere else."

She felt a stab of pain deep in her guts. Her liver and spleen, spots on her lungs—what was left for the cancer to eat? The stab did not just come and go. Suddenly it was difficult to breathe. Kevin stood and came over and sat beside her. There was a glass of water beside her bed. He held out a handful of white pills.

"Morphine," he said. "Spence gave them to me. Two is a lot."

"I think I need two." She took the pills from him and swallowed them down with the help of the water. "Thank you. I guess it's hard drugs from here on out. I can forget about the herbs."

"You tried, that's what counts," Kevin said.

"I refused to accept reality, that's what counts."

"Ilonka."

"I know, I'm not so terrible. But I'm not so great, either, and I always thought I was. I wonder if other people think about their lives the way I did. I would look around and see all the mistakes others were making, and I thought I wasn't going to be so foolish. I was going to make my mark on the world. But look at me now. A handful of people know my name. A handful of people know I'm dying, and then when I am dead, even that handful will forget."

"I won't forget."

She smiled faintly. "You'll remember me on the other side? I hope so. Maybe you'll be an angel and come for me when I leave the body to fit me with my wings."

"I don't know if Herme ever had wings or not."

"You know, Anya really wanted you to finish your story last night. I think she knew she was going to die." When Kevin didn't respond, she hastily added, "I didn't say that to make you feel guilty.

Your story is just so captivating." She took his hand. "It's midnight, can't you tell me the final installment of 'The Magic Mirror'?"

"But Spence isn't here."

"You can tell him the rest later," Ilonka said.

Kevin thought for a moment. "Maybe I should finish the story now." He pointed to her glass. "May I have a sip of your water first?"

"Of course."

Kevin had his drink of water and made himself more comfortable on her bed, borrowing one of her pillows to prop himself up. He seemed to have no strength left in his back, in any part of his body. He cleared his throat and began. His voice came out soft and dry. Ilonka suspected he was taking plenty of morphine.

"Herme left the bridge where he had come close to suicide, but he didn't go home. There seemed no point in doing so. He walked the streets until dawn, which was not that far off, and then decided that he was going to find a job unrelated to art. He felt that by continuing to paint he was still living in the narrow world he had in the museum, and even though he was hoping to get back to the joy he had experienced as an angel, he also wanted to go beyond that. He believed God had granted his wish to be mortal because God had wanted him to become more than he was. Herme decided to embrace life, in all ways.

"He decided to become a taxi driver. The only problem was he didn't have a driver's license. He did have a fake American passport that Teresa had purchased for him on the black market in Paris before they had entered America. With that he was able to get a temporary license, and then a job as a taxi driver. The company put him on the night shift, which was all right with him. Driving a taxi in New York City is hard work. There is the constant fighting with traffic and strange people. But that was the one thing Herme loved—all the different people he met. Living with Teresa he had been somewhat sheltered from the world. As a taxi driver he was face to face with the best and the worst the world had to offer.

"He stayed in New York for five years, and in all that time he never ran into Teresa. Over time the pain of what had happened eased, yet he never went through a day without wondering how she was. He still loved her, you see, but he was never tempted to try to find her because he could see that his love for her was not enough. She still had to live her life and grow her own way, just as he had to. He saw that he was actually bad for her in many ways. He had made her dependent on him, and likewise, he had become needy. But he wished her well, Herme did, he wished everyone well. There wasn't a person who rode with him that didn't leave him feeling a bit better. That was enough for him. That he could work at a job and give love to complete strangers each day. He wondered sometimes if that was why everyone was on earth—just to learn how to give love constantly.

"But after those five years he left New York City and moved to Colorado, to live in the Rocky Mountains. He became a forest ranger in a national park, and when he was not on duty, he would often hike deep into the forest and camp out under the stars at night. He craved the wilderness, the solitude, yet there was also a part of him that remained lonely, still searching, maybe for that perfect human companion, maybe for something else.

"There was this one woman who also worked at the national park that he liked. Her name was Debra, and she was the cutest thing, at least to Herme. They spent time together, and it wasn't long before she moved in with him. For Debra being with Herme was like a dream—he was the kindest man imaginable, also one of the funniest. In the many years since leaving the Louvre, Herme had developed an incredible sense of humor. One day, after living with Herme for six months, Debra asked him to marry her. Herme was flattered and not good at saying no. So a date was set, and at long last Herme was going to be married.

"A week before the wedding a huge fire broke out and Herme was sent in to fight it in a remote part of the forest, where he found a family trapped by the circling flames. Bravely, he broke through the wall of fire to the people, and immediately the wall closed behind him. But Herme found the only way out for the family—they had to scale down the rocky side of a sheer drop. Initially the family was frightened to do what he said, but as the flames closed in they changed their minds. Herme had a rope and other climbing gear and he helped the woman and children down first. It was when he was coming back up for the man that he ran into trouble. The wind had changed and the fire was precariously close. It reached his rope, and when Herme was halfway up the cliff it started to smoke. He could see the rope burning above him and tried to grab on to the rocky cliffside for support. But it wasn't enough, and when the rope burned through he fell a hundred feet to the ground. He landed on a boulder and his back was broken.

"He didn't regain consciousness for a couple of days, and by then he was in a hospital in Denver. Debra was by his side, and he learned that the man on the hill had not survived the fire. He also learned that he was to be paralyzed from the waist down for the rest of his life. Herme took the news badly because one of his greatest joys as a mortal was in being able to move around and *feel* the earth, something he had been denied as an angel.

Debra was devoted—she promised to stay with him no matter what. Yet Herme didn't feel a crippled husband was something she should have to live with. Although it broke his heart to do so, he refused to see her. She would call and write to him during his convalescence, but he continued to ignore her. In time she gave up, and once more Herme was alone.

"He was down but not out. In time he was discharged from the hospital and able to get around in a wheelchair. The staff at the hospital had left a lasting impression on him, and he decided he would like to be a doctor. It was a momentous decision because he was older and as a paraplegic his life expectancy was shorter than ordinary. Plus he had to start his schooling from the beginning. He had to attend college for four years before he could apply to medical school. Fortunately, during all this time, he received money from the state because he had been injured on the job.

"But Herme was determined, and after nine years of struggle he was officially a doctor. He had massive debts from medical school but he immediately began to work in a free clinic, which offered services to the poor and homeless. By this time he was living in Los Angeles, in a crummy apartment with a broken-down elevator that could hardly carry his wheelchair to the top floor. But he was content, maybe not as happy as he had been during the days immediately after he left the Louvre, but satisfied that he was performing a service to humanity. His main difficulty was his health. People in wheelchairs often have trouble with their kidneys, and Herme had not been working many years as a doctor when his began to fail. Part of the problem was his own laziness. He was so busy taking care of others that he failed to watch his diet and drink enough fluids. In time he had to go onto dialysis, and this slowed him down some. Yet he continued to work long hours, even as his hair turned white and began to fall out. As an ex-angel he was not afraid of death, yet he felt if he were to die soon, it would be with regret. But he didn't know why. He had done the best he could with his life.

"He was ready to leave the clinic one night when a woman, close to death, was brought in. It seemed she had been living on the streets and had a severe case of pneumonia. She was literally drowning from the congestion in her chest. Herme examined her and drew a blood sample. She was clothed in rags and covered with dirt. For those reasons, and also because she was completely emaciated with numerous sores on her face, he didn't recognize her. But after the nurses cleaned her up he saw that it was Teresa.

"He was overjoyed to be with her again, yet saddened because she was obviously very ill and he could tell her life had not been easy. She was half delirious, and he immediately started her on medication. Fortunately the pneumonia responded to the drugs, and within a day her temperature was down. But it didn't go away, and after more tests he knew she had a full-blown case of AIDS. Her pneumonia was not bacterial, but a parasitic type that is common in AIDS patients. He realized she was going to die and that there was nothing he could do to save her.

"While working in the clinic he wore a nametag, but it only had his last name, which he had invented, so she had no idea who he was. Herme was both saddened and relieved by her lack of recognition. He was sad because he had never forgotten her, and felt he must not have mattered much to her since he had passed out of her memory. Of course, he knew he didn't look like the young man who had walked so boldly from the Louvre. At the same time he was relieved she didn't know him because he didn't know what he would have said to her as the great love of his past. They had not parted under ideal circumstances.

"He continued to take care of her, though, often staying after his shift was through to do special things for her: rub her back and bring her the paper, and buy her books and bring her tapes to listen to. With her fever down, she became talkative again, and was always pleasant to him. But it was obvious that she was in a great deal of pain, and also suffering from depression. As the days passed he was able to get her to open up and talk about her life. He learned that she had been married twice and had two children, but that both her marriages had ended badly and that one of her children had been killed in a car accident. It seemed that the death of the child had started her on a downward spiral from which she had never been able to escape. She had become addicted to alcohol and lost her job and then her house, and then everything, and had ended up on the streets. Herme almost wept as she talked, thinking how it could have been if they had stayed together, especially when she mentioned someone special from her youth. Then he realized he had been too quick to judge her memory.

"'I met him in Paris,' she told Herme. 'When I was a young woman. He worked at the Louvre, that famous museum with all the da Vincis and Raphaels. He was an artist and I fell in love with him at first sight. He was so shy when we met—I practically had to twist his arm to get him to leave the museum. From the beginning we were inseparable. He got a job painting portraits and soon he was able to open a studio. We lived together and he took good care of me. Then we moved to New York City and everything went wrong. He didn't want to paint portraits anymore and we were getting low on money and I was getting nervous. Then I met another man and had an affair with him. Well, the inevitable happened, my boyfriend came home and found us together.' Teresa sighed. 'He turned around and walked out and I never saw him again.'

"Teresa's talking about the fateful night brought it all back to Herme. He just stared at her, unsure what to say. Yet he realized that he did not blame her for what had happened, and that reassured him.

"'The memory is a painful one for you,' he said gently.

"She sniffed. 'I never had a chance to tell him how sorry I was for what I did to him, and how wonderful he was.' She smiled suddenly. 'Did I tell you about his talent? The pictures he painted—they took people's breath away. He could have been one of the greatest artists in the world. Over the years I always kept an eye open for his work. I kept expecting to see it, but I don't know what happened to him.' Her smile vanished.

"'What's the matter?' Herme asked.

"'Nothing.' Then she began to cry. 'Doctor, I tell you all these things but I can't even remember what I was like in those days.'

"'I'm sure you were very beautiful.'

"'I don't know.'

"'Maybe you will meet him again and be able to tell him how you feel.'

"She shook her head. 'I don't want to meet him looking this way.' Abruptly she stopped and scanned her surroundings. 'How come there's no mirror in this room?' she asked.

"There was no mirror because Herme had removed it while she had been delirious with fever. He hadn't wanted her to wake up and see how devastated her features had become with her skin cancer. He remembered how vain she had been. Also, because of her treatments, her hair was falling out, and she was almost completely bald. He put off her request for a mirror but she was insistent. Finally he agreed to bring her one the following day. As he stood up to leave, she stopped him.

"'Am I seriously ill, Doctor?' she asked."

"'Yes.'

"'Am I going to die?'

"He hesitated. 'I'm not sure. We're doing the best we can. Only God knows.'

"She closed her eyes and nodded. 'That's something my boyfriend always used to say. Only God knows. It was his answer to everything. It irritated me at the time, but now I think it was a good answer.' She opened her eyes. 'Thank you, Doctor.'

" 'Thank you, Teresa.'

"She smiled. 'For what?'

" 'For everything,' he said.

"That night, on the way home, Herme stopped at an art-supply store and bought: paints, brushes, a sketchpad, a couple of canvases, and an easel. He hadn't painted in decades, but as he set up the tools in his tiny apartment he felt a rush of power and exhilaration. His talent had not left him, he felt. He knew he was about to create the greatest work he had ever made. He set to work painting Teresa as she had appeared to him the first day he saw her. He worked throughout the night, not stopping until it was time for him to return to the clinic.

"There he was met with a shock. Teresa's condition had suddenly worsened and she was near death. He rushed to her side and tried to awaken her, but it was clear she was slipping into a coma. The other doctors at the clinic told him to forget her. But he refused, staying by her side throughout the day and that night, holding her hand. His painting was leaning against the wall, still wrapped up and waiting for her to see. Herme had not prayed to God in a long time for anything, but that day and night he prayed with all his heart. That she should not die not knowing that she had been the most beautiful thing in all creation to him. That she still was.

"In the morning, at dawn, she awoke and opened her eyes.

"'Doctor?' she whispered. 'Have you been here long? Have I been asleep long?'

"'We've both been asleep most of our lives, Teresa. I brought you a mirror. Would you like to see it?'

"Teresa nodded and Herme held up the painting for her to see. As he did so, she saw her youth and the very essence of her life unveiled before her. A light shone on her face. She stared at herself as a young woman, and then at Herme, and it was as if all her life was revealed there in that moment, in that room, and it hadn't been so bad. It was magical what happened, a magical moment in the eternity of time.

"'Herme,' she said and embraced him. 'My love.'

"'Teresa,' he said, holding her tight."

Kevin paused. "She slipped back into her coma not long after that and died later that same day."

Ilonka had tears on her face. "What became of Herme?"

"I don't know."

"I understand." He was saying he *was* Herme, and he wasn't sure what was going to happen next. She leaned over and kissed him briefly on the lips and hugged him. "It was the best."

He was pleased. "Really?"

"You are the best. Did I ever tell you?"

"No. Did I ever tell you that you're pretty all right yourself?"

175

She laughed. "Just all right?"

He smiled, holding on to her. "You are special to me."

She sat back. "Can I ask you a few things about your story?"

"If you let me ask you a few things about your stories."

"It's a deal. You said one of the reasons you told that story was for me. I won't ask you to explain that since you already refused, but I couldn't help noticing that certain members of the Midnight Club seemed to be in your story either symbolically or really. There was the wheelchair, which naturally reminded me of Anya. There was your talent for painting. There was the thing of doctors taking care of dying people. What I want to know is if *everything* in your story was relevant to the members of the Midnight Club?"

She was asking because she wanted to know if he knew about Anya's experience with Bill, which had an uncanny parallel to what happened with Herme and Teresa. Also, despite what she had just told him, she wanted to know how much of Teresa was supposed to be her. Finally she wanted to know if there were things about the others in the story that she did not know. Unfortunately Kevin's response was not helpful.

"The story unfolded naturally in my mind. I didn't consciously try to include each member of the group, but I suppose subconsciously I might have, since I knew they would be the only audience for the story."

"That's another thing that's sad, that this story

should just die with us here. I wish it could be recorded and distributed, maybe even published."

"Neither of us has the strength to write it down. And what about your stories? They deserve to be recorded as well. They are wonderful tales of morality and nobility."

"Now you're exaggerating," she said, although she was flattered.

"I'm serious. They meant a lot to me, Ilonka."

She laughed again. "Only because you think you're the hero in each of them."

"I never said that."

"Oh, you did in your own elusive way." She paused thoughtfully. "And maybe you were the characters that I thought I was. Delius and Padma were certainly more together than Shradha and Dharma, and you are certainly more together than me."

"I won't argue with that."

"You!" She shoved him gently, never too hard.

"Ilonka," he said, giving a mock cringe at her touch.

She grabbed his hands. "I love to hear you say my name." She stopped. It was here, she could feel it—the moment of truth. It didn't have to be a big deal, though. Really, she thought, she preferred it like this, a quiet affair late at night in her room. "I guess you must know by now that I love a lot more than that."

He acted innocent. "Huh?"

She pulled his hands close to her heart. "In each of my stories there was always you and I. It doesn't matter who was who. For me you have always been there, Kevin, even before I met you." A tear fell from one eye and she let go of him long enough to wipe it away. "God, this is embarrassing. I don't want to start crying now."

"Don't." He wiped the tear away for her. "You don't have to say anything. That's the beauty of meeting in the middle of the story. We already know each other."

She couldn't stop crying. "But I just wanted to tell you before it's too late. I just wanted to hear the words." She leaned over and kissed him. "I love you, Kevin."

"I love you, Ilonka. You know that."

"I didn't know that."

"Well, now you do." He lifted her chin because it had begun to droop again. "Why are you still crying, sillyhead? Are you expecting me to give you a big yellow gem? Are you expecting me to unveil a stunning painting of you? I'm sorry, but I don't have anything in the pockets of this robe except morphine and Kleenex."

She had to chuckle even though she started crying again a second later. She pressed his hands to her mouth and kissed them tenderly, bowing her head to him, too ashamed to expose her real self to him, and too afraid that she would never have another chance.

"I'm afraid to die unloved," she said, weeping. "And I know you just said you loved me and I believe you. But I need more than that and there isn't time for more. Since I first saw you I wanted to love you, really love you. Do you understand what I'm saying? I wanted to sleep beside you and feel you close to me. I wanted to *make* love to you, Kevin. I've never done that in my life and now I never will." She shook her head and tried to pull back. "Oh, God, I can't believe I'm saying these things to you. You must think I'm a pathetic creature."

"Yes," he said.

"I know that I am."

"No. I mean, yes, let's make love. I'll stay with you tonight."

She almost fell off the bed. "You will?"

"I would be honored to."

He had shut her up quick. She was stunned. "But, I mean, can we? My abdomen is pretty scarred, and Dr. White says I have tumors bigger than oranges inside me."

"Are you scared?" Kevin asked.

"Yes. I'm bald."

"What?"

"This is a wig. I have no hair. Chemo killed it."

"I know."

"You know?" She was astounded.

"Yes," Kevin said. "But that doesn't matter. I'm scared, too. I'm in worse shape than you. I can't even walk up a flight of stairs. But none of that matters. We can make love without having sex. We can take off our clothes and hold each other and it will be better than in the movies." He pulled her into his arms and kissed her on the lips, slow and deep. Then he whispered in her ear, "I won't hurt you, you won't hurt me."

"Will you get cold without your clothes on?"

"You'll keep me warm."

"You won't die during the night?" It wasn't the best question to ask, but it was a fact she feared. But for once her love was stronger than her fear. She pulled him close before he could answer and said, "No. That won't happen. I won't let you die."

It was a promise she made to him.

She *had* made him other promises—in the past, or maybe just in the land of imagination where things often were more real than reality itself. He had made her promises as well, but who knew? Maybe both their dreams were just "wishes come true" in another time, another dimension. As she slept in Kevin's arms, a jumble of *possible* lives exploded in Ilonka's mind. Most were simple fragments: a scene of her walking as an old man in a rice field; a glimpse of herself as a child running through a daisy-filled meadow. Others were of bizarre days: herself as an alien being traveling to other worlds in a spacecraft and collecting beings and subjecting them to experiments, some painless, others fatal; herself as a mermaid-like being that lived in an underwater city marvelously developed and complex.

The main thing about all these lives was that in each one she knew a bit more, and didn't make *exactly* the same mistakes—although she had a tendency to repeat certain patterns. Yet, from the perspective of that highest part of herself that could be called the soul, they were all happening at the same time. Everything was happening in the eternal moment, and that was the one place she refused to be. She was always looking ahead to something that might be better, longing for it, or else stuck in the past, worrying about what could have been. The one thing she never did in any of her lives was live fully in the present.

She was always longing to be loved.

She saw a life, more than a glimpse really, where she was a powerful king married to a devoted queen. This was in the land of Lemuria, the great continent in the Pacific that sank beneath the waters even before Atlantis reached the pinnacle of its civilization. She was happy until she met a woman whom some said was capable of bringing the highest delight, and others said was a witch. But she was intrigued with this woman—as a king, *he* was intrigued. His queen became aware of his fascination and told him about the woman and let him make his own decision about whether to go to her.

"She is not a witch and she is not an angel," the queen said. "She is an ordinary mortal woman. But she knows a secret that enables her to bring the most pleasure to a man. It is called *Rapture*. In the sex act pleasure is confined to a small part of the body. But in Rapture, slowly, through a cunning sequence of caresses, the entire nervous system is brought to a climax. It brings two thousand times the joy, and two thousand times the loss of vitality. All her men become addicted to her, and will never leave her. All her men are like thralls and have no minds of their own. They sleep all day and their only thought is when she will come to them again. But if you want to go to her, go. Even though she will give you physical delights it will never make you forget what you have here, which is my love."

So he went to the enchantress, this master of Rapture, and she was glad to have him. Because even though she had many admirers, she had to struggle to get by, and here was the king of the land showing an interest in her. He resisted her seductions, wanting to get to know her better and wanting to see if she really was as formidable as he had heard. This was a peculiar quality of the king—he liked to stand close to danger, believing that he always had the wisdom and power to pull free at the last moment. And he was a powerful man and very intelligent, and the enchantress saw that and was impressed. She had never met a man who was able to resist her for even one day, and this king stayed with her many days without sleeping with her. Indeed, after more than a week he finally came to her and said, "It has been nice to spend time with you, but I am going back to my wife. I miss her."

At this the enchantress was stunned. "But you have never even slept with me. How can you leave?"

The king laughed at her boldness. "What is this thing you do that I hear so much about?"

She smiled. "Oh, it is just love. How can you flee from love?"

The king was not fooled. "I do not feel around you what I feel around my wife, which is true love." But then he added, because he did find her fascinating, "But maybe another time we will meet and I will know the full pleasure of your company."

At this the enchantress smiled slyly because she knew that the seeds of the moment were capable of becoming the fruit of tomorrow. "We will meet, and on that day I will be the master and you will beg to stay with me."

The king acknowledged her proud words with a bow, although he thought she was wrong. "Perhaps" was all he said.

He returned to his queen and lived happily ever after.

But then, almost instantaneously in Ilonka's slumbering mind, *he* was born again in a Scandinavian country in the Middle Ages as a poor milkmaid, suffering from a disease that made *her* completely bald from birth. Life was painful for her, with little joy. She lived as an outcast because many believed her presence brought bad luck. When she was sixteen years of age, however, she met a young man and fell in love with him. But although he treated her kindly and with respect, and was never afraid to be with her, he did not share her affection. That fact caused her untold grief. Never had she wanted anything as much as she did this boy, and she prayed to God to give him to her no matter the cost. But her prayer was filled with a feverishness and a lack of concern for what was best for the young man. So as a result it was cursed, even though her prayer was granted for a short time.

A wizard came into her life, a man who could start fires with the mere wave of his hand, and whose gaze was as cold as the harshest winter. This wizard was attracted to her because even though she was an outcast and far from charming in appearance she had a pure soul. That purity drew him like a powerful fragrance. He wished to use her for his own aims. He saw her as the light source he could use to power his most vicious spells. He came to her as she knelt in a stone church and prayed for God to bring the boy of her dreams to her arms. There, in that church, he taught her the most wicked part of all black magic—*Seedling*. He promised her the boy would soon be hers.

Seedling was related to Rapture in that it used the sex drive to compel people to act against their wills. But it was far more subtle and dangerous. Rapture was completely physical, while Seedling dominated through psychic deceit. With Seedling she was able to draw the boy to her whenever it suited her, which was often. But she didn't just use her newfound power to get the boy, but other men as well because anyone who used Seedling quickly became promiscuous. They, in fact, became addicted to what they were forcing on others.

For this *gift* the wizard wanted something in return, and at first that was her instant availability whenever he wished her. This she granted, although it repulsed her to be in his arms, especially right after seeing the boy she loved. For she really did love the boy, although she used him in the worst way imaginable. She sensed that she had known him from *before*. It was her love for the boy that made her question what she was doing. These questions came to her at the same time the wizard placed a great demand upon her. He ordered her to use her special powers to attract a certain count and seduce him, and then, while the man was asleep in her arms, to cut his throat. The count was an old enemy of the wizard and was the wizard's obstacle to power. She agreed to do as he requested because she was so afraid of the wizard, but once out of his sight she hurried to the church and prayed to God to free her from the wizard's influence. She begged that her evil power be taken from her.

While she prayed the boy she loved came by, and with tears in her eyes she confessed everything. Even though the boy had been used by her, he loved her now. Indeed, he would have eventually fallen in love with her even if she had never used Seedling on him. He forgave her and suggested that they should run away together. The prospect excited her and she hurried home to gather her things for the journey. While she was packing the wizard appeared and cursed her for betraying him. She pleaded for mercy, but he showed her none. He stabbed her with the same knife he had given to her to use on his enemy. He left her for dead, lying in a pool of blood.

Before she died the boy found her and pulled the knife from her abdomen. It was an evil blade that had been forged with spells and dipped in poison. The girl knew she was going to die, and she wept how she had thrown away her life and love. But he told her not to worry, that one day, in another time and place, they would be together again. This he promised her, but the girl had doubts because of all the wrongs she had committed. Then the boy made her another promise.

"I will share your wrongs," he said. "So that wherever fate places us we can be together. Even if it should mean our future days will be dark and filled with pain. Because even in that darkness our love will be in the light."

Those were the last words she heard before she died.

Her dreams, her nightmares, her visions—all wrapped together. Ilonka stirred uneasily in her sleep and instinctively reached out for Kevin's arms, experiencing a repeat of the episode with the wizard as she felt a stab of pain in her lower abdomen. It was not a blade that hurt her, however, but her cancer. Yet it was possible there was a connection between what had been and what now was.

In any case, she felt relief as she pulled Kevin closer. Her mixed collage of the past brightened and cast a ray over her future. In that light she saw Herme the angel painting a blue-white star that shone in a starry heaven. She stood at his shoulder as he worked, as if she were his personal muse, and she felt hope staring at his work, yet she did not know why. She only knew that one day she would journey to that star.

Ilonka slept the remainder of the night wrapped in the warmth of that hope.

And she dreamed no more.

In the morning she awoke with Kevin lying asleep beside her. The sun shone in through her open window, which surprised her because she thought it had been closed when they went to bed. A fresh ocean breeze played gently with the curtains, but it was not as cold as she would have expected. It was warm and sweet, as if they had skipped the fall and winter in the space of one night and come to an early spring. A bird sat singing on the windowsill and Ilonka waved to it. At the gesture the bird paused and stared quizzically at the two of them as if trying to decide which one to continue singing for. Ilonka smiled and pointed to Kevin and the bird sang some more. It was then that Kevin opened his eyes.

"Is that you?" he asked.

She leaned over and kissed him. Before she had fallen asleep, she had kissed him a lot. "Yes, my darling boy. I told you I have a beautiful voice."

He smiled at her. "What a beautiful sight to wake up to." He closed his eyes and sighed. His face was very thin. "What a beautiful sound."

She ran her hand through his fine hair. "Did you dream last night?"

"Yes. About you."

"So did I. It was nice, but I'm glad it's morning."

"So am I."

"I love you, Kevin."

"I love you, Ilonka."

He never did open his eyes again, dying a few minutes later in her arms.

CHAPTER VIII

TWO DAYS LATER ILONKA WAS AT THE EDGE OF THE cliff throwing Kevin's ashes into the wind and the ocean. She didn't sing as she had told him she would, at least not out loud, but there was a song in her heart. She was satisfied that she had told him how she felt before he left the world. It also meant a great deal to her that he had felt the same way.

Kevin's parents had no objection to her dealing with his remains, especially since he had left a written request to that effect. Ilonka finally got to talk to them. They were nice people, the mother especially. The woman naturally was grief stricken over the loss of her only child, yet her grief seemed equaled by the relief that her boy was no longer suffering. Ilonka had written an apology to Kathy and gave it to Kevin's mother to give to the girl. In the card Ilonka said that Kevin had died peacefully. Dr. White had told no one where Kevin had taken his last breath.

Dr. White did another favor for Ilonka. He put

her in touch with an old friend of Anya's—a guy named Shizam. Ilonka called him and explained how she wanted to get hold of Anya's old boyfriend, Bill. Shizam promised her he would do what he could to find him.

Sandra also called and Ilonka talked to her. Sandra was back in high school, trying to catch up on the work she had missed. Although they spoke at length, they didn't say much that was significant. Their worlds were too different—Sandra was rediscovering hers and Ilonka was losing even the hospice she called home. Her health was failing swiftly now. Ilonka wondered, as she talked to her, if the reason Sandra had never been able to tell a story was because she had never really belonged to the club, if it truly had been only for the dying. Their precious Midnight Club—would there ever be another?

Probably not in this world.

Ilonka had little contact with Spence after Kevin's death because they were both feeling so ill they spent all their time in their rooms. Spence had contracted a severe case of pneumonia that could kill him. The staff did nothing to treat him; they just kept him as comfortable as possible. Ilonka's own comfort was costing her six grams of morphine a day, and even that didn't stop the pain entirely. But she bore it patiently, there was nothing else to do.

A day arrived—it was almost two weeks after Kevin's departure—that Dr. White came to her room and told her that Spence was near death and wanted to talk to her. Dr. White took her down to Spence's room in a wheelchair and left her alone with the Midnight Club's one and only wild man. Spence's new roommate was at a group meeting. Dr. White had yet to assign a new roommate to Ilonka, for which she was grateful. She found herself craving solitude as her time ticked down.

Spence looked awful and she told him so and he said as much about her. They laughed softly over their predicaments, they were so hopeless. Actually, though, Spence's appearance did shock her. In the short time they had spent apart he had developed a severe case of what looked like skin cancer on his face and arms. It made her wonder, many things. He was having a terrible time breathing. They had him propped up with so many pillows he looked like a stuffed skeleton.

"Hey, when are we going to Hawaii?" Ilonka asked.

"I've been saying all along that I'm ready when you are."

"Yeah, but you never come across with the airline tickets."

"You can't squeeze blood out of a turnip."

She laughed. "Is that an old saying or did you just make it up?"

He scratched his head. His hair was very thin as well. "I honestly can't remember."

A silence settled between them. Ilonka was not troubled by it. Maybe it was all the morphine she was taking or maybe it was just that she had finally come to terms with her impending death, and nothing could disturb her now. Yet she still had many questions left in her mind.

"What can I do for you, my dear friend?" she asked finally.

He raised an eyebrow. "You assume I want something from you? Maybe I just wanted to enjoy your company for a few minutes." He paused. "There were a few things I wanted to talk to you about."

"Fire away."

"Did Kevin tell you the final installment of his story before he died? I know he spent his last night with you."

"Who told you that?"

"No one. I figured it out for myself. He wasn't here."

She nodded. "Yes. He did tell me what became of Herme and Teresa. Would you like to hear?"

"Yes. Very much."

She told him the third part as best she could remember. When she was done Spence smiled.

"That was a nice touch there at the end," he said. "I was wondering why he called it 'The Magic Mirror.'"

The retelling of the story had brought back to Ilonka the many similarities the characters in the tale had to the people in their club.

"But we want the blood ceremony."

"You can have it if you want. I'm going to bed."

"Is there a story you want to tell me?" she asked carefully.

"What do you mean?"

"About the night Anya died?"

He was suddenly wary. "What about it?"

"How did she die?"

"She had cancer."

"We all have cancer, Spence. I remember something odd about that night. I had taken a long nap that afternoon and yet I was hardly able to make it back to my room after we were done with our stories."

"So?"

"I also remember how when you went to pour my glass of wine you suddenly stopped and got another glass. You said there was dust in it." She paused. "But I didn't notice any dust."

"The glass was filthy," Spence said.

"Oh, I think my glass did have something in it. But I think it was the *second* glass. Come on, Spence, what did you drug me with, and why?"

"You have a wild imagination. You've been listening to too many preposterous stories."

"Don't B.S. me. There was a drug in my wine."

"Why did you drink it if you thought there was something in it?"

"Because I am a stupid Polish girl. Answer my questions, please."

He sighed. "Phenobarbital. One gram. I spread it in a fine coat around the inside of the glass."

"Why?"

"I can't tell you why. I promised not to."

"You don't have to tell me. I know already. You

wanted me out cold so that you could help Anya end her life."

"You said it, I didn't."

"And I notice that you don't deny it. What puzzles me, though, is how she died. Dr. White said it couldn't have been a drug overdose. Certainly she didn't shoot herself." She spread her hands. "What happened?"

"Does it matter? She's dead. Let her rest in peace."

"I don't ask for her sake. Nor do I ask out of curiosity, even though I am curious. I ask for your sake."

Spence chuckled. "Don't worry about me."

"I do worry about you. You're my friend, and something is troubling you. It doesn't take a psychologist to see that. Your stories were amusing—a hundred people blown away every night. At the same time they had a common theme: rage against society, the establishment. Where does all that rage come from?"

"You said it, you're not a psychologist. Don't dissect me."

"Why did Anya chose *you* to help end her life?"

"I didn't say that I did help her."

"Why hasn't your girlfriend ever shown up?"

"She couldn't afford the train fare."

"Why do you have sores all over your face?"

Spence suddenly flared up. "Because I'm dying, dammit! Leave me alone."

Ilonka nodded. "You are mad about it, aren't you? I was mad, too." She leaned over and touched his hand. "I care about you, Spence. I'm not here to torment you."

He shook off her touch. "Why are you here?"

"You asked me to come. You wanted to talk to me about more than Kevin's story." She stopped. "What are you dying of, Spence?"

He drew in a shaky breath and nervously rubbed his hands together. When he looked at her there was so much pain in his eyes it almost broke her heart.

"Why do you ask when it's clear you know?" he said. "I have AIDS."

"Did you catch it from Caroline?"

He swallowed. "His name was Carl."

"It's all right. You don't have to be ashamed."

"What do you know about what I have to be ashamed about?" he shouted.

She wheeled herself closer and grabbed his hand. "Tell me."

He shook his head pitifully. "This isn't story-time."

"Yes it is, Spence. It may be early morning for the rest of the time zone, but it's close to midnight for us. They're going to turn out the light soon. This will be the last chance we get to talk. This will probably be the last chance you get to talk to anybody. So what if you're gay? That's nothing to be ashamed of. It never was anything to be ashamed of."

Spence coughed. "That's so easy for you to say. But this day and age is not that far removed from the Middle Ages when you're in high school. Yes, I am gay—have been since I was born. Don't try to probe for a reason why. There isn't one. My parents didn't molest me when I was young, and I wasn't exposed to radiation from your local nuclear powerplant. You can admit being gay if you're famous or live in the right part of the country, or even if you're older. But when you're a teenager you have to hide it and don't try to tell me that you don't. In my school fags were fags, they were not people. And I wanted to be a person, Ilonka. I am a person."

"You are one of the greatest people I know."

"Only because you don't know me that well. Who was Carl? He was the love of my life. I met him when I was fifteen. He *was* a great person. He would do anything for anybody. He was as brilliant as Kevin. When I met him it was like finding a life preserver in the middle of a turbulent ocean. I clung to him that tightly, and that was fine because it didn't make him love me any less."

"I'm happy you were able to find someone special," Ilonka said.

Spence gestured helplessly. "A couple of years ago I went for an AIDS test. I thought I should get checked out. I'd had a lover before Carl. Well, to make a long story short, I tested positive."

"I see."

"I didn't tell Carl."

"Why not?"

There were tears in his eyes. "Because I loved him and I was afraid I would lose him if he knew I was sick. Don't you see what I did? I loved him and I killed him!"

"He's dead? But who's been sending you all these letters?"

"I write them and mail them to myself," he whispered.

"You don't know if you killed him. He might have given you the disease."

"I doubt it. Carl was never promiscuous."

"You don't know," Ilonka insisted.

"That's just it. I don't know. I will never know. But I can't stop thinking about how he looked the week before he died. He looked like something that should be burned and buried." Spence pointed to the mirror on the far wall. "He looked like me."

"I'm sorry."

"That's what I told him! But it was too late." Spence buried his face in his hands. "The worst thing was he never blamed me."

"Even if you did give it to him, by the time you found out you had the virus it was probably too late." She reached over and hugged him and he slipped into her arms, tears running over his cheeks. There was so little of him left, of either of them. She couldn't remember the last time she had eaten a meal. "You have to let it go. You can't die tormenting yourself like this."

"I've tried. I can't let it go. What I did—who could forgive me?"

"But he forgave you."

He buried his face in her chest. "It's too late.

There are no words you can say that will make things better for me. I am going to die this way. I deserve to die."

She stroked his head. "I had a dream last night. I was a witch who controlled a young man, and the ironic thing was I loved the guy. I'm not sure, but I think it was Kevin. Anyway, there was this evil wizard and he stabbed me in the guts, and I was bleeding to death when this guy found me. I had done nothing but use the guy and still he loved me. As I was bleeding to death he told me we would meet again, either in heaven or on earth in a future life. But I doubted his words. I didn't think I could be with him because of the awful things I had done. But he told me something just before I died that stayed with me as I crossed into the other world. He said that if I had indeed done something wrong, then he was willing to share the consequences of that action with me so that wherever we went, we would go there together. I honestly think that's why Kevin was here with me. I don't think he deserved to be here, I think he chose to come to teach me what I had to learn. To teach me what the Master has been trying to teach me in every life."

Spence raised his head. "What is that?"

"It will sound corny if I say it."

Spence reached for a Kleenex and blew his nose. "I'm in a corny mood."

"I think I am here—we are all here—to learn divine love. To love the way God loves us."

Spence coughed. "If God loves us so much, why did he invent AIDS?"

"If you had not caught AIDS I would not have a chance to make you the offer I am going to now."

"What is that?"

"If you honestly feel you have done something so terrible that you cannot be forgiven, then I am willing to share your sins with you. When we die, if we should have to stand before God and be judged, then I will tell him I am as much to blame as you and that half your punishment should be portioned out to me."

Spence was incredulous. "I don't think you can do that."

"Kevin did it."

"That was just a dream."

"I think this whole world is just a dream."

"That's all that morphine you're taking."

"Are you accepting my offer or not?" she asked.

"Why are you making it?"

"Because I love you, Spence. You're my buddy."

"Do you really think God is going to judge us together?"

"No. I added that part for effect. But I do think you should stop judging yourself. But if you can't, I accept that." She grinned. "We'll both go to hell together."

Spence brightened. "Think of the stories they must tell down there."

"I imagine the Midnight Club is always in session."

Spence reached over and embraced her. He kissed her on the cheek. "It means a lot to me, what you say. Maybe there is magic in your dreams.

Kevin kept telling me there was. I do feel better being able to share my burden with you. I always wanted to tell you."

"Did Kevin know?"

"I didn't tell him, but I think he guessed. He was very perceptive. Anya knew, though."

"You told her."

"She knew Carl. They lived in the same neighborhood." Spence released her and sat back. "I smothered her to death. She asked me to."

"She couldn't stand the pain?"

Spence sighed. "It was bad for her at the end. The morphine couldn't stop her agony. She told me that I was the only one who could kill her because of what I felt I had done to Carl. She said it matter-of-factly, not in a cruel way. I understood what she meant—I didn't hold it against her." He shrugged. "I guess everything gets easier the second time around."

"It wasn't easy for you."

Spence nodded. "It was worse than you can imagine. I took her pillow and pressed it down over her face and I could hear her smothering—with you sleeping peacefully only three feet away. I had to keep telling myself that I was just giving back to her the thing I had stolen from Carl. I know that doesn't make a lot of sense, but even more than his life I felt like I had taken Carl's dignity from him. He did not die easily. Anya told me that she wanted to go out with a little dignity. I could give her that much."

"You did a very brave thing."

"You think God will see it that way?" He genuinely wanted her opinion.

"He will probably give us time off our time in hell because of it."

Spence finally smiled. "Then after that we'll probably be reincarnated as penguins in that part of Antarctica where the ozone layer is completely wrecked. I'll have skin cancer all over again."

"Who took Anya's toiletries?"

The question stopped him. "I don't know."

"Spence. Don't lie to me."

"I suspect Kevin took them. After I returned to my room, after I had killed Anya, Kevin got up and left. I was surprised because with his leg it was hard for him to get around. He told me he had something he had to do. He knew I had drugged you and that I had just smothered Anya. You couldn't hide anything from that guy. Anyway, I think he took her stuff."

"But why would he want to delude me?"

"You said it yourself in that story you told about Delius and Shradha. The only comfort Shradha had after the death of her child was that her daughter had come back for her things."

"But that never happened," she protested.

"I know that. Kevin knew that. But until your Master told Shradha the truth, she was quite happy with the delusion. Kevin wanted to ease the trauma of Anya's death for you, and also allow you to go to your own death with the belief that there was something on the other side."

"I already believed that."

"But Kevin said you were still afraid."

"That's true." Ilonka considered a moment, then laughed. "Kevin *did* think he was Delius, and that I was Shradha. That rat—he kept denying it."

"He wasn't trying to hurt you."

Ilonka sighed. "I know that. He couldn't hurt a soul."

Spence enjoyed her pun. "Do you have any other questions?"

"No."

"Every mystery is solved?"

"No. The big mystery will not be solved until the day we die. We have our stories, our dreams, our beliefs, but until then everything is just speculation."

Spence coughed. "We will not have to speculate much longer."

Ilonka smiled sadly. "That is true."

CHAPTER IX

MORE DAYS CREPT BY. FOR ILONKA THEY WERE LIKE
one long ride through a dark tunnel where she kept
imagining—maybe the word was *praying*—that
there was a light at the end. Her pain worsened and
it got so that she couldn't even get out of bed. Dr.
White visited her daily. He continued to let her live
alone in her room. She supposed he figured it
wouldn't be long. He brought her white Swiss
chocolate—it was the only thing she could eat.
Four tiny squares a day—she let it dissolve in her
mouth and then took a sip of water. Tasted better
than the herbs had.

One afternoon when she was just lying there as
usual a knock came at her door.

"Come in," she said softly.

A strange young man stepped in the room.

*"When I first saw him, I thought he looked funny.
His hair was a weird orange color and he wore an
earring that looked as if it had been stolen from an
African native."*

"Bill," Ilonka said with pleasure. The guy had not changed his style.

He appeared uneasy. "A friend of mine gave me a message that you were looking for me."

"Yes." Ilonka tried to sit up as best she could. Moving was agony. She had to take a breath before she could speak again. "I was a friend of Anya Zimmerman's. Did your friend tell you she's dead?"

His cheek twitched, but otherwise he gave no sign of how he felt. "Yes."

"She was my roommate. She told me about you guys—how you met, how it ended. You can sit down if you want. That was her bed."

"All right." Bill glanced at the bed nervously before putting his bottom on it.

"Like I said, she told me how things got messed up between you guys. She was crying when she told me."

Bill showed interest. He was a handsome guy, his hair color notwithstanding. He had a sharp look in his eyes. Ilonka remembered Anya had said he wanted to be a detective.

"I guess it didn't work out for her with the other guy," Bill said diplomatically.

"The other guy was nothing to her. Anya didn't even know what she was doing with him. She was happy with you. But you know how sometimes when you're the happiest you begin to feel like you don't deserve it? Then you do something to screw it all up?"

"I've never done that, but I understand what you are saying."

"I hope so because I'm saying it badly. What I mean is, Anya loved you and was sorry for what happened. She wanted to tell you that before she died but she was too sick and too ashamed."

Bill's lower lip suddenly trembled and he bit it. "I appreciate you telling me that." He paused and touched the bed hesitantly with his palm. "Did she suffer a lot?"

"Yes. But in the end she was with friends. That helped."

"I wish I could have helped her," Bill said with feeling.

Ilonka smiled. "She left a box of stuff. Dr. White—he runs this place—didn't know what to do with it. It's on the floor of the closet there. Please take it. I know she'd want you to have it."

Bill took out the box and set it on the bed. The first thing he removed was the small clay statue Anya had been making to give him on Valentine's Day. The two unpainted lovers holding hands. Bill held it up without a sign of recognition. Ilonka supposed he couldn't remember more than the main highlights from that particular night.

But Ilonka remembered.

"I said the only part he broke was my right leg."

Yet the statue was whole. The girl's right leg was in place.

Ilonka gasped. "Give me that."

Bill hastily handed it over. Ilonka studied the statue closely.

There was no sign of repair work.

It was as if the leg had *always* been there.

"What is it?" Bill asked, worried.

"It's a sign," Ilonka whispered.

"What are you talking about?"

"Bill. You know how people say time heals all wounds?"

"Yes."

"Well, what if time ran out? Do you think love could heal what was left?"

"I'd like to think so. Hey, what's so special about those two clay figures?"

Ilonka closed her eyes and hugged the statue to her heart.

"Death couldn't tear them apart," she said. "Death couldn't touch them."

Eventually Bill left, with the statue; she felt it belonged to him. He left but the miracle remained. Ilonka tried to call Spence to tell him what had happened but Dr. White told her he had slipped into a coma. She was sad to hear the news, but her sorrow she now accepted as readily as her joy. It didn't seem she could have one without the other. She lay back in her bed and rested.

A day and night went by. Dr. White came and told her that Spence was dead. Three down and one to go, she thought. What a story it all would have made. She cried at the news but not for long. She was so tired.

Then time lost its meaning to her and she drifted on calm waters down the long tunnel. The sun rose and set. The earth turned. She breathed in and out, more shallow, though, each day more softly.

Finally a morning came when the sun streamed through her open window and the ocean breeze stirred her parted curtains. She awoke to the sound of a bird singing. The white dove sat on her windowsill staring at her, and as Ilonka looked over, the bird turned its head toward the sun. Ilonka followed its gaze and was surprised to see a bright blue star in the sky, even with the sun's rays burning down. The star shone like a jewel of incomparable worth. For a long time Ilonka stared at it, and as she did so, one by one, more stars appeared in the sky, until soon the whole of heaven was lit with points of light that did not twinkle, even as her eyes began to tire and blink. The entire galaxy shone in all its glory, even as the sun grew brighter and brighter, and her eyes slowly closed for the last time.

— *EPILOGUE* —

THE STARLINER *SPACE BEAGLE III* WAS SCHEDULED
to depart for Sirus in less than one hour.
Eisokna stood high up in space on the observation deck of the great ship and stared
down at the blue white of earth. The sun shone
brilliantly off to her left. The stars were all
around. Earth had been her home for all the days
of her life, but now she was leaving it with her
husband, probably for good, and the knowledge
filled her with both sorrow and exhilaration.

She pressed her nose to the clear plastic that
separated her from the vacuum. Her breath flared
around her on the hard material with a ghostly
fog; it was cool on the observation deck. With
Karlen, whom she had only recently wed, she had
worked hard to be able to go on this journey.

To be one of the first settlers to colonize Treta, the sixth planet in the Sirus star system. They were realizing the dream of a lifetime, she knew, and the best thing about it was that they were doing it together. Yet she was sad because she wanted to say goodbye to her world, to thank it for what it had given her, and she didn't know how.

Suddenly, as she stood there still as a statue, she thought she heard a bird singing. A wave of nostalgia swept over her, so powerful it brought water to her eyes. A tear touched the clear plastic and momentarily blurred her view of earth. Where was the sound of that bird coming from? It sounded as if it were singing in her ear, such a beautiful melody.

A strong, warm arm wrapped around her from behind.

She relaxed into it. Karlen kissed her on the nape of her neck.

"Ready to leave?" he asked.

She sniffed. "I don't know. I was standing here looking at the earth and I felt as if I were saying goodbye to my best friend. But I also felt as if everything was finally settled between us, and now I can move on. Do you know what I mean?"

Karlen moved to her side and hugged her close. "No," he said, but he smiled.

She laughed; he always made her laugh. "I don't either. You're supposed to be my best friend." Wiping away her tears, she leaned over and kissed him. She was happy; it felt as if it had been a long time coming and she was determined to enjoy it. The sound of the singing bird faded into the distance and was gone. "Yes. I'm ready to leave."

Look for Christopher Pike's
The Last Vampire
Coming in May 1994

---

finally. Wiping away her tears, she looked over and closed her eyes. It was almost, if not quite, had made one, encompassing and inescapable to enjoy it. The sound of the singing bird faded into the distance and was no more.

Look for Christopher Pike's
Fall Into Darkness
Coming in May 1990

CHRISTOPHER PIKE was born in Brooklyn, New York, but grew up in Los Angeles, where he lives to this day. Prior to becoming a writer, he worked in a factory, painted houses, and programmed computers. His hobbies include astronomy, meditating, running, playing with his nieces and nephews, and making sure his books are prominently displayed in local bookstores. He is the author of *Last Act, Spellbound, Gimme a Kiss, Remember Me, Scavenger Hunt, Final Friends* 1, 2, and 3, *Fall into Darkness, See You Later, Witch, Die Softly, Bury Me Deep, Whisper of Death, Chain Letter 2: The Ancient Evil, Master of Murder, Monster, Road to Nowhere, The Eternal Enemy, The Immortal, The Wicked Heart,* and *The Midnight Club,* all available from Archway Paperbacks. *Slumber Party, Weekend, Chain Letter,* and *Sati*— an adult novel about a very unusual lady—are also by Mr. Pike.